Urban

Hathaway House, Book 21

Dale Mayer

URBAN: HATHAWAY HOUSE, BOOK 21
Beverly Dale Mayer
Valley Publishing Ltd.

ISBN-13: 978-1-773367-83-5
Print Edition

Books in This Series

About This Book

Welcome to Hathaway House. Rehab Center. Safe Haven. Second chance at life and love.

Urban's arrival at Hathaway House was as painful and as unexpected as possible. He'd been placed here with Lance's help, after Urban suddenly lost his spot in his current center. Still scarred and injured, Urban should be happy to have what help he could, but, for the first time, he realizes that he wants to be more than *as good as he can be*—for someone very special at Hathaway House. Too bad his scars are so ugly …

Bettina felt her heartstrings tugged by Urban's struggle to sit, to work, to make something of his life. He is such a mix of personalities that he continually surprises her by his overall good humor. However, he struggles to be with others because of his facial scars.

She refuses to accept that. He needs to see how wonderful he is, regardless of the war wounds he is left with. Now to get him to believe it …

U RBAN CHADWICK STARED at the inside of the ambulance. He hadn't really expected to be making a trip this soon, but apparently other people had plans. He was not allowed to remain where he had been any longer. Supposedly he'd outlived his stay, and it had more to do with the numbers and the time frame that he'd been booked for. He'd had another center to go to, but that transfer had fallen through. Now he was headed to some place called Hathaway House. He wasn't even sure how he'd gotten in, but he'd called an old friend of his, and that had been their answer.

Thankfully Hathaway House had had a bed for Urban.

So here he was, good to go, in theory. Now, in reality, if only his back would allow him to survive. And then there were the scars—the real reason why he hated to go to new places and to meet new people. His face, neck, and, well, the rest of him, usually put people off.

He had never gotten used to it. Plus the journey to Hathaway House itself was painful, but at least he was lying down, which was better than sitting up. He couldn't sit for long, and he had a lot more rehab ahead of him. But, according to Lance, this place was the best of the best.

Urban rolled his head to stare out the little bit of a window that he could see, but the vehicle's flashing lights were driving him crazy, along with a headache. He closed his eyes and prayed the transfer would be over soon.

The attendant by his side said, "Hey, this is an easy transfer, only on the road for an hour."

Urban nodded. "Yep, I hear you. Just wish I knew where I was going."

"You'll be in heaven," the attendant said.

At that, Urban's eyelids flew open, and he rolled his head ever-so-slightly to look at him. "What do you mean?"

"I've heard absolutely nothing but great stuff about Hathaway House," the attendant said, "and we've taken some of the most broken bodies there. I've seen several of them walking around the streets months later, and I've been in shock."

Urban stared at him hopefully. "Seriously?"

"When you're there, and you get a chance," he said, "look it up. Their success stories. They are pretty amazing."

As they hit another pothole, Urban closed his eyelids, his whole body shuddering in reaction.

"Apparently one of the PT guys there has done a lot of work on stability," the attendant shared. "I think that'll be what you need."

"I need a lot more than that," Urban admitted. "That hip replacement was not exactly an easy surgery."

"If you'd had a normal hip joint for them to replace, it might have," the attendant said. "Instead of that, you're dealing with recovery from multiple things. You will be in the best hands there."

"I hear you, and hopefully this is the place to get past all that."

"It is," the attendant said. "Not to worry."

"I sure hope so." With that, Urban winced and just endured.

Chapter 1

URBAN CHADWICK STARED at the small room around him. As far as accommodations went, this one was pretty high-class. And he was sure happy to be here, if only because the trip itself was over. He'd had multiple people come talk to him, but none of it was making much of a dent. The pain had been pretty severe, so he'd been given painkillers almost immediately. And he knew now it was a matter of more time just to get him to adjust to being here and to recover from the journey.

At that thought, yet another person walked in, took one look, and nodded. "Hi, I'm Shane."

"Nice to meet you," Urban managed, trying to breathe through the pain.

Shane noted his grimace. "But you'd rather talk to me at any other time, right?"

"It's the pain. ... I'm waiting for the pills to kick in."

"Yeah, and the journey would have been rough too. You've got a couple days to yourself to feel a bit more normal," Shane pointed out. "Then we'll start running you through some tests."

"*Great*," Urban muttered, "I can't wait."

Shane laughed at his dour tone. "And I know you don't necessarily want to be here, nobody in your situation wants to be anywhere," he admitted, "but we're here to help."

"I hope so," Urban replied. "There was a mix-up at the other center, where I was supposed to go," he explained, "and somehow they didn't have a bed for me anymore."

"Lucky for you, now you're here," Shane stated. "Lance pulled some strings to get you in."

"I appreciate it. I wasn't sure where I would end up. For a while I was afraid I'd end up on the streets."

"Nope, not happening. And, from the looks of it, not a moment too soon. Your last surgery was what?" Shane flicked through his tablet. "Hip replacement. Interesting."

"Not really. Most of it was shot off," Urban told him. "I took a bunch of shrapnel, and that pulverized the bone. An attack we never saw coming. They tried to replace my hip, and it worked to some extent, but we kept having bone spurs. The scars all over my body were just the icing on top."

"Right. The scars are the minor issue here. Big for you in terms of appearance but maybe less in terms of functionality. So the bone spurs, did the doctors go in and scrape them off?"

"They did what they could, yeah," he said, "but the joint itself was too far damaged. So they rebuilt the hip socket and put a new ball on the end of the femur."

"Good enough," Shane noted, "and I can see you've got some back issues too."

"Yeah, what made you say that?" he quipped in a dry tone.

Shane's lips quirked. "Your pain for one, and you're not relaxed. You look tight and tense."

"I'm pretty relaxed. ... I always look that way. It's the scars."

"Nope, you're holding yourself stiff, guarding against further injuries still."

"After the journey, maybe that's to be expected."

"Maybe. We'll see what we can do about it," Shane stated. "I won't push you for a couple days, so that we can get some of that inflammation back down again. However, then we'll run you through the gambit and see what we can do for you."

"And, if there's nothing you can do, will I get moved again?"

Shane looked at him in surprise and shook his head. "Nope, you're here for the duration. We'll do a lot and plan on getting you back on your feet."

"That would be lovely," he agreed. "I do find it very hard to sit for long periods of time."

"Yeah, I can see that. The damage is pretty extensive," Shane shared, "so we'll start with some strengthening exercises and a lot of pool work."

"Pool's good. I'm a good swimmer—if for no other reason than I know I can drop and relax without pain."

"Precisely. The pool exercises will help stretch out some of the scar tissue as well," Shane explained. "So rest up, and we'll see you later." At that, Shane almost walked into the woman standing behind him.

As she stepped forward, she asked Urban, "Did those painkillers kick in yet?"

"No, not yet," he shared, "hopefully soon though."

"I brought them in for you, and I want to confirm that we've given you the right dose." She added, "I've got your chart. I want to update it and make sure we've got all the current medications listed."

"Did my chart come with me?"

"It did," she said, "but I handle dispensing medication, and I don't take any chances." When he stared at her silently, she shrugged. "It'll still be on me to ensure that you don't have any adverse reactions, and I want to know what I'm dealing with."

"I get that. It's just a surprise."

"Around here there'll be a lot of surprises," she stated cheerfully, "and it's all good."

"What's your name?" he asked.

"Bettina," she replied, looking up and smiling. "My family's German."

"Is that a German name?" he asked, with an odd look. "I wouldn't have known."

"Yep, it's a German name," she confirmed. "And nobody would expect you to know. And not to worry about the noise, as all the chatter around here will calm down soon."

"I can't wait," he murmured.

"Yep, and, if you run out of medication," she said, "I'm on for the entire night shift."

"Will do," he replied.

She placed the buzzer in his hand. "Just ring me when you need to." And, with that, her voice, ever so soft and gentle, dropped yet a little more. "Sleep. I'll talk to you about food and sustenance afterward."

She closed the door for him, and, in no time, he drifted off to sleep.

BETTINA WROTE DOWN a note on his condition. He was more exhausted than a lot of them who came in. And he also appeared to be in deep pain. His body was soaked in sweat, and his forehead was creased. The scars on the right side of his face and neck were red and angry. She'd seen that in stressed patients before. She would return in a couple hours and see how he was doing and get his bedding changed, if needed. The last thing she wanted was somebody to catch cold while lying in the sweat and still recuperating. Especially when the painkillers could knock him out pretty hard.

She wrote down several notes for herself and headed back to her desk. She quickly updated everything and continued her normal routine. She came on at 4:00 p.m. every day. A lot of people were surprised she even liked the night shift, but she'd been doing it for long enough that it was fine. And, for the next couple hours, she was more than busy. By the time she stopped for dinner, most of the dining room had cleared out.

Dennis looked up, smiled at her, and teased, "If you take your dinner too much later, you'll miss out."

"Then I'll just grab something from the coolers," she said, with a smile.

"How are things?"

"It's good, just, you know, busy."

"Always busy," Dennis murmured.

"And we got a new patient today," she shared. "His arrival was later than we expected."

"I haven't seen anybody new for dinner," Dennis noted, one eyebrow raised.

"No, and he's asleep right now. The trip was pretty rough. I might need to call on somebody here to get him some food in a bit."

"Not a problem," Dennis stated. "I have some really good leftovers here, if you want me to put a plate away for him."

She looked at the food and stared. "It's hard to know what he might want. I also don't know if he has a touchy stomach."

"If I make him up a plate, he can eat it or not," Dennis suggested. And, with that, he grabbed an empty plate and served up some of the roast chicken and vegetables.

"Make sure you add in some carbs to that," she added. "He's pretty lean."

"He probably is not getting much down, especially if he's in that much pain," Dennis guessed.

"In this case it's quite possible. Also the scar tissue on his face and neck might be a factor affecting his food intake. Plus there was a mix-up with his original transfer, and he lost his bed elsewhere because of it. Lance apparently got him in here."

Dennis nodded. "Good for Lance, and the new guy just doesn't know it, but it was a lucky mistake."

She chuckled. "We'll do our best to convince him of that." Just then her pager buzzed. "Speak of the devil," she murmured. "That's him now."

Dennis glanced at the plate in his hand and then at her.

She nodded. "Just put it off to the side. I'll be right back."

"But you haven't eaten either."

"Nope, I haven't, but let me go check on him." And she picked up the pace and raced out of the dining room.

Chapter 2

B ETTINA KNOCKED ON Urban's closed door when she got there and heard his voice call out something, but it was a little indistinct. Still, she assumed that it was okay to go in. She poked her head around the door and asked, "Hey, you need me?"

He turned to her, and his eyes were glazed over.

"Aah, pain's pretty bad, *huh*?"

"Yes," he gasped. "It's really awful."

She checked his medications and frowned because he'd had all the pain meds that he was allotted. "Let me talk to one of the doctors." And she quickly dashed down the hall, checking to see if Dr. Robertson was still in his office. He was just packing up to leave, but Bettina explained the situation. He nodded and checked the chart she held out. He quickly assigned another painkiller for Urban to go along with what he'd already taken.

Bettina retrieved the added dose and entered Urban's room, holding up the pill and a glass of water. "One of the doctors was still here."

Urban nodded slowly. "Good. It might be tough to get more down on an empty stomach though."

"Let's give you this first," she suggested, "to take the edge off, and then I will bring you something to eat." And that's what they did. When she returned with the plate of roast chicken, he frowned at it. "I didn't even ask you what you wanted. I had mentioned to Dennis, the guy who runs our dining room," she explained, "that you were new here. So he saved this plate for you."

"It looks wonderful." Still Urban hesitated.

"Come on. Let's adjust the bed, so you can sit up and eat." And she showed him how the bed worked. Some of these beds were modern; some of them were older. This one happened to be quite a new one, so it was easy to maneuver.

With him sitting up somewhat, he added, "I'm probably good like this for maybe half an hour, but my back won't take much longer."

"Your half hour then is to eat," she said. "I have dinner waiting for me as well. So, if you're okay to eat right now, I'll come back as soon as I've finished."

"Go," he replied. "And if you're getting the same thing I'm getting, you definitely don't want it to go to waste."

Bettina chuckled. "No, we don't want any food here wasted. Every meal here is to die for." And, with that, she took off running.

URBAN LISTENED TO her footsteps bemusedly. Did she always run from point A to point B? He would have to find out, but it might take a bit to understand all the nuances around here and how everything worked. So far, outside of the pain of his arrival, the food in front of him was doing a lot to make him feel like maybe he'd ended up in a decent spot after all.

He tasted the roast chicken and closed his eyes, chewing slowly. He was afraid of *too*-too much food in his stomach, mixing with the painkillers, but, man, that was a rough journey over here. And shouldn't have been but, with all the road construction going on, it seemed as if there was absolutely no end to the pain going on in his world. And he was tired of it. But, hey, he was here, and he would make the best of it. Hopefully something positive would happen in the progress department.

He wasn't at all sure what to think about Shane, but, as long as he could help, Urban was willing to go through the paces. He knew it wouldn't be easy; none of this rehab stuff was easy. He'd been injured before, but not like this. And this was a one-way street out of his career, so he must rebuild everything. And yet all he cared about was making sure his body was back to as good as he could make it. And, if that wouldn't happen, everything else would be rough.

It was all about focusing on priorities, and right now the priority was making it back to as healthy as he could be. Sitting for longer periods would be good, and, heck, getting back on his feet would be absolutely divine. To walk again? … Yeah, that's what he was talking about.

When he slowly replaced the knife and fork on his tray, he realized that he'd eaten 90 percent of the food. There was no dessert with it, which he also thought was interesting. However, his dinner delivery was not exactly normal. She'd grabbed him something, and he appreciated the fact that any food was even left for him. He'd been at some centers where it would have been a cold sandwich at this hour. When he heard footsteps racing toward him, he already knew it would be Bettina.

When she poked her head around his doorway, he smiled at her. "I heard your footsteps. I think there's only one speed that you go, and that's top speed."

She chuckled. "You're not the first person to mention that. However, it always seems to be just what I need to do in order to get moving. Things are busy here."

"I get that."

She walked in and checked his dinner plate. "I'm really happy to see this," she said, pointing to his tray. "I'm delighted that you managed to get so much down."

"I just hope it isn't too much," he whispered. "I don't know about the medications here, but sometimes they don't react all that well when food is added."

"Let's hope tonight is fine," she noted, "but remember. If you need anything, I'm here all night."

"I was wondering …" He hesitated.

"What do you want?" she asked, as she quickly stacked everything onto the tray.

"Is there any chance of a coffee?"

"Oh my goodness, of course, and I know a few pieces of dessert are in the cafeteria, if you want something else."

"I'd love something to go with the coffee," he said. "I was thinking that I was already too full, but just the thought of having something sweet would, I mean, psychologically, make me feel much better."

At that, she burst out laughing, and her laughter was so infectious that he couldn't help but grin at her. Then felt the pull of the tight skin on the side of his face, and his laugher fell away.

"I hear you there," she noted. "I have to really watch it. Otherwise I'll gain twenty pounds on my job here," she murmured. "The food is included for us as well. Dennis and Ilse—she's the head chef—whenever they get going, I tell you something magical happens. The food here can be quite something. Let me go see what I can find." And, with, that she disappeared again.

She wasn't running this time with the tray, but her pace was amazingly fast.

Urban settled back on the bed and noted that, so far, the pain in his back hadn't kicked in. For that, he was grateful. If he could even have a little bit of time free of pain, it would be nice. Most people didn't realize just how debilitating constant pain was and how it completely knocked you flat on your back, until you couldn't do anything.

He wasn't a whiner, and he was never anybody who thought that the pain could be quite so bad, but this time? Well, he'd learned a lot about himself and about the limits the human body could tolerate and yet how much it could come back from. It constantly amazed him. He was just sad that the healing journey had to be something he experienced. He would have been quite okay to never deal with any injuries of this nature again.

Instead, here he was, and that's just the way it was.

He reminded himself to just enjoy the peacefulness of being here and the sense of relief in having this stage of the journey over and avoiding the panic about not having a place to go. When he heard a knock on the door, he opened his eyes to see her standing there.

"I didn't want to wake you," Bettina whispered.

"Honestly, I'm just mellowing out right now," he murmured. "Do you know the relief I feel in having this day over?"

"And getting a good night's sleep," she stated, "will be huge." She walked closer and placed a large mug of coffee near him. "I forgot to ask if you wanted anything in it, so I brought cream and sugar."

But his gaze had locked on the piece of cake in her hand.

"And this is Devil's Food cake," she announced with a big smile, placing it on the little table beside him. "If that appeals."

"How could something like that not appeal?" he asked, staring at it in amazement. "It looks delicious. I know it's probably a cake mix, but, man, they sure make it look good."

"No cake mixes here," she declared, with a smirk. "I know Ilse makes her own mixes, and she keeps things like that on hand, but you won't find a box around here."

"You serious?" He stared at her in surprise.

"Very serious," she replied. "Now remember. I'm here all night. If you need me, call me."

"Oh, if I wake up, I will," he stated. "Chances are the pain will jerk me awake, once the painkillers stop working."

"If that's the case, we'll give you some more. Don't you worry. That pain won't help you heal," she stated. "Only with relief from pain can you lift your head and figure out where your progress is at."

He smiled and nodded. "Most people are happy to give you the drugs just to keep you compliant."

"Compliance won't be part of your remedy here," she countered. "This is very much a case of you being active in your own recovery. And, for that, we need you awake. So we must get the pain down. Then we can get you to work better."

She was saying all the right things, yet he just didn't know how any of it would work.

Long after she had gone, Urban felt the drowsiness kicking in, even as he sipped his coffee. If he wanted cake, he should eat it now because, man, oh man, his eyelids were getting pretty heavy.

Chapter 3

BETTINA CHECKED IN on him several more times that shift, yet he slept like a log all through the night. She knew he would wake up screaming in agony in the morning, but, for the moment, he was sleeping well, and that was worth everything. When she met with her morning replacements, she filled them in on Urban's arrival and what he'd been given.

"Now I'm warning you," she said to Susan. "He's likely to wake up in absolute agony. I did just check on him ten minutes ago, but he's still out."

"I'll make him first on my list," Susan promised.

And, with that, Bettina headed home to her apartment here on the grounds. She was tired and concerned about Urban because he was new, different, and the transport hadn't been terribly easy. He was appealing in an oddly endearing way. The scar tissue had calmed down as he relaxed, not looking quite so angry. Sometimes they had patients arriving, and it was a walk in the park. Other times it took four to five days for some patients to recuperate just from the trip.

She had witnessed many where they had to go right back to the hospital because the recovery didn't happen here or they'd injured themselves in the transfer. Some people came by car. Some people came by ambulance, and some people came in friend's vehicles because that was the only way they could get here. And each came with its own challenges.

In Urban's case he appeared to have trouble sitting for long periods of time, so he'd been lying flat on a stretcher. However, that in itself hurt him every time the ambulance hit potholes. And honestly, Dallas had so much construction on an ongoing basis that she was amazed that anything ever got finished.

As she walked into her place, she quickly had a shower and then went to the pool. It was early morning, but it was perfect because nobody was here. She would need to sleep, but she had to unwind first. Then she would probably have breakfast because she hadn't had a whole lot of dinner last night herself.

Her nighttime shift, although calm, had been busy. And busy was good because then she didn't get bored. Yet she had been keyed up for every waking minute, expecting to be contacted by Urban. When that hadn't happened, she constantly found herself detouring to check up on him. The fact that he'd slept was absolutely huge for him, but, for her, it was almost like a let-down.

She'd been waiting for that buzzer notification from him every time, and it never came. That had been a stressor itself. But, even now, as she floated in the water, trying to decompress, she couldn't stop thinking about him. Something was unusual about him that just caught her sideways and seemed to hang on.

Bettina didn't know whether it was the circumstances or just his politeness or knowing he was another person in need. She didn't know him yet, but he was special. With a smile at her silliness, she rolled over and started doing laps. She could float for a while, but, in order to really unwind, she needed to burn off some of that energy.

Urban was right; she seemed to have only one speed, and it was at a top-notch level at that. She'd always been like that, and sometimes that nervous energy took over and took her a while to unwind. But here, right now, at this place? She handled it better than she ever did. Which was a good thing because here she was trying to do so much for other people that it was easy to forget about looking after herself too.

That's not something she wanted to deal with. Not now. She'd already spent way too much of her lifetime recuperating from her own issues that she sure didn't want to get caught up in that space again. Most people here didn't know that she had been anorexic, when she was a child, a young teen. It had taken her years to overcome her emotional issues and to eat enough. And now she forced herself to eat, even when she wasn't hungry.

But she also had to worry that she wouldn't come back to the same problem. So she made sure that food was something she made time for on a regular basis. And, so far, she'd been holding herself to do that quite decently. It had been five years since her last issue. Still, five years just wasn't quite long enough for her to feel comfortable enough to think that she was over it.

Still, watching other people here have much bigger issues to deal with went a long way for her to keep her life on track. These veterans had serious problems to deal with. Hers were minor, and, as long as she reminded herself that she could handle anything, it all worked.

After her swim, she quickly threw on her cover-up and then walked to the dining room. She was still a little damp, but it was good. As long as there would be some food soon, she would eat, and then she would go to sleep. She walked in, one of the first, grabbed a tray, snagged a fresh hot coffee, feeling a bit of a chill because her hair was still wet, and then stepped into line.

Dennis took one look and smiled. "You were in the pool today, weren't you?"

She smiled. "Yep, now I need some hot food to warm back up."

"Got it. What's your fancy?"

"Pancakes," she replied immediately, seeing a fresh stack come out. "I'll definitely take some of those." And, with pancakes, bacon, and eggs, she headed for the deck outside, where she could sit in the sun and dry off. All around her, she heard the staff, who had come in early for breakfast, talking about the roster. But she needed to detach from all of it, just find something else to think about. Yet the only thing on her mind was Urban.

She looked over and saw Susan getting coffee. Bettina called out to her, "Hey, Susan. Did he wake up?"

Susan smiled and detoured to Bettina's table and said, "Yeah, he's awake. I just gave him his pain meds, and this coffee's for him."

"Good," Bettina replied, as she got up, taking her tray to the trolley. "I'm glad he's awake. I'll stop by and see him."

Immediately Susan handed the cup to her. "Why don't you take it to him?"

She frowned. "I don't want to interfere."

"Hey, he was asking about you already." Susan gave Bettina a fat smile and held out the cup again.

"Ah, in that case"—Bettina grabbed the coffee—"and he takes it black too." With that, she walked to his room, poked her head inside, and said, "Hey, stranger."

He looked up in surprise. "I thought you were off shift."

"I was." She pointed at her head. "The wet hair gives away that I just came from the pool."

His eyes widened. "Wow, what a way to start the day. I'm really looking forward to doing that, now that I know there *is* a pool." He laughed.

She smiled. "Yep, as soon as you're doing better."

And then he frowned. "I think Shane mentioned something about a pool last night."

"Probably," she agreed, "and, if he mentioned it, you'll get there a whole lot faster."

"Hope so," he murmured. "The pools are a lot easier on my system."

"Not a problem. Part of the protocol. Here's your coffee, and now I will go head for a nap," she said. "And you know who to call, if you have a problem."

"Not you," he teased.

"Maybe, if you have a problem getting hold of anybody, then don't hesitate."

"No, go on," he said. "You need to get some sleep."

"I'll see you tonight," she replied, and, with a lift of her hand, she turned and walked away.

URBAN DIDN'T SEE Bettina again until several days later. He was just coming back from rehab with Shane, sagged onto his bed, when he heard a sudden noise and looked up.

"Hey, I did knock." She smiled at him. "I don't think you heard me."

He nodded. "That's all right. I'm kind of dead today."

"Sorry," she said sympathetically. "Was it testing today?"

He looked over at her and groaned. "Is this a normal

thing for everyone to be so exhausted afterward?"

"Not so much a normal thing but it's to be expected," she replied, as she stepped in closer. She frowned as she studied him. "You look really exhausted. Do you want me to get you a bite to eat to go with this cup of coffee?"

"I was thinking about breakfast," he admitted, "but it's too far to go."

"I can handle that quite easily enough," she said, "but what would you like to eat?"

He laughed. "I think everybody here is just bound and determined to feed me."

"Food is an essential part of your healing process. Let me go see if any treats are out. You do have a sweet tooth, right?"

"Right. I don't think anybody *doesn't* have a sweet tooth," he stated, with a smile. She was as lovely to look at as she was a help to him. "And thank you."

"You would be surprised to hear that a few people actually turn away dessert." She shook her head at that. "Now drink that coffee and sit, relax, and forget about the testing for now."

"Thank heavens," he muttered. "Who knew that you could be tested for so many things?"

"Shane is very thorough," she declared, "and his methods get results."

"And that's why I didn't complain." Urban massaged his scarred neck. "It's still hard."

"It is, indeed." And, with a wave, she disappeared.

He had expected to see her later that day, but, when she didn't show, he finally realized that maybe she was just busy or was off or something. He hadn't been bothered about it or asked anybody about it, but, at the same time, he'd wondered where she'd gone. He was determined to ask her when she got back.

And, indeed, as she came back a couple days later, holding a small plate in her hand and a tube of something in the other, he greeted her by saying, "And how dare you leave me for the last couple days. I could have had this dessert delivery every day."

She burst out laughing. "You're absolutely right, and I'm sorry. And, of course, nobody told you that I was sick, did they?" He frowned at her. She smiled. "I woke up with a sore throat, and, one of the things that we're always very careful about here is that we don't bring any germs into work," she explained. "So I ended up taking two days of sick leave. I should have texted you."

"Oh, not at all," Urban replied. "I just wondered what happened."

"And that's what happened." She held out the tube in her hand. "This is a special cream for the scarred skin. It's nice to know I was missed."

"Of course you were missed," he stated cheerfully. "However, I did spend most of those two days just resting and not doing a whole lot." He looked at the tube curiously but didn't open it. He wondered at her impulse to get such a thing. The burn unit had given him an ointment and later other moisturizers to keep up the treatment.

"Resting is part of what you're supposed to do," she noted, with approval. "Sometimes people try to overdo rehab because they're here, and they think they need to jump in and grab this with both hands and make the best of it. However, too often they end up right back in the hospital."

Urban stared at her in horror. "Now *that* would be enough to make me stop putting in too much effort at all.

The last thing I want to do is go back into the hospital."

"That's pretty well what everybody says," she agreed, with a nod. "And I understand that. So just stay chill, stay calm, follow everybody's instructions, and they won't guide you wrong."

"Well," he began, then laughed, "I know one thing. You guys won't let me starve." He eyed the treat she'd placed on the small table beside him. "I don't even know what that is."

"I think it's a fresh raspberry cheesecake," she said, looking at it. "I should have grabbed a piece for myself too. By the time I get down there again, none will be left."

He offered, "Have mine."

"Nope, not at all. That's for you. I have to go get dinner yet anyway."

"Ah." He nodded. "Are you coming on shift then?"

"I am," she confirmed. "So I'll be here for the evening. If you don't want to make your way down for dinner, let me know, and I'll get you something." He hesitated, so she added a stern warning, "And I mean that. The worst thing you can do is overdo your rehab *and* not eat properly."

"All Shane did was more testing," he shared. "It doesn't feel very good to know that *just testing* will finish me off like this."

"But wouldn't you rather know now," she murmured, "than find out later, when you're even more susceptible to problems?"

He shook his head. "I'll see. I'll have my coffee, get a shower, and then consider how I feel."

"You do that. If you need a hand, you know where I am." As she walked to the doorway, she looked back at him. "And use the cream. It will help with the tightness." And, with that, she was gone.

He hadn't even considered what would happen if somebody here got sick, but, of course, the patients all had compromised immune systems, and every one of them in this building struggled with something. Therefore, it made sense that none of the staff were allowed inside with illnesses. As he was new, most people didn't know that he was even curious or worried about her. Something else he hadn't even considered.

Such a strange feeling to be in a place where everybody seemed to be so friendly. People had been friendly before, but it was a different kind of friendliness here. He could feel that they meant it. Didn't say a whole lot for where he'd been before at this rate, but it confirmed a lot about where he was now, and, for that, he was grateful.

He settled back to enjoy his coffee and relax. He had to admit to wondering whether he should go down for food or not. He knew she was sincere, but, at the same time, he figured she probably had more-than-enough work to keep her busy without him bugging for something like dinner. By the time he had coffee and a shower though, he was getting shaky again. He looked at the treat, ate half of it, and then sat back and wondered what was the right thing to do.

Just then Dani showed up, spied the cheesecake, and her eyebrows shot up. "So, have you already made it down for dinner?"

"No," he replied, "but Bettina popped in, saw that I wasn't in very good shape after all the tests Shane put me through today. So, she grabbed me a coffee. And, of course, with the coffee, she came back with this."

"I'll have to go make sure I get a piece," she noted enviously. "I will tell you that the cooks around this place prepare food that is to die for."

He laughed. "You hired them, so that's kudos to you."

"It's kudos to them. We would be lost without them."

"Oh, it seems as if everybody's been here for a long time," he noted, "or at least I get that impression from listening in on conversations."

"Our staff has been a godsend," Dani murmured. "Don't know what we'd do without them."

"Hopefully you never have to find out." He smiled.

"Right? That would be deadly. Now," she asked, "how are you settling in?"

He shrugged. "I mean, it's early yet. I just spent another day testing with Shane. Somehow I assumed that testing meant that it would be an easy day."

She burst out laughing. "A word of warning, there's no such thing as an easy day with Shane. He's on a mission to ensure that you're the best you can be."

"And I am more than happy to hear that," Urban stated, "but it does mean I wasn't quite prepared for what *testing* would mean."

"And you need to tell him if it's too much, whether testing or rehab," she said seriously. "He will absolutely listen to you."

"But then," Urban added, "if it *isn't* too much, I'll lose out on some of the benefits by not working as hard."

She frowned as she studied him. "One of the hardest things we often have to do is tell people to hold back," she shared. "I get that everybody is desperate for progress, and they want to be the best they can be. Believe me. I understand that. I just don't want you getting hurt, overstressing, or putting your body through too much, especially before it's ready."

He hesitated because, of course, that was similar to what

he'd already been told. He slowly nodded. "Got it," he muttered. "And you're right. It is hard because we do want the best, and we want it now."

"And you're hungry for it," she stated, with a smile. "And that's good. At the same time, you need to pace yourself."

"Right," he murmured. "Pacing isn't exactly something I'm well known for."

She burst out laughing. "I don't think any of you guys are," she declared affectionately. "You all come here with these agendas in your head, not necessarily agendas that work out for the rest of your body."

He had to grin at that. "True enough."

Chapter 4

WHEN BETTINA HEADED down later that evening to grab a cup of coffee, she was surprised to see a lone person sitting on the deck. She looked over at Dennis, who was wiping down counters. "How long has he been there?"

"Quite a while," he replied. "I was just about to go ask him if he was okay, if he needed a hand getting back."

She nodded. "I'll do that." She walked over and sat down beside him. "Hey."

Urban smiled. "Hey back."

"How're you holding up?"

"I ended up falling asleep and not coming down for dinner. When I did show up, Dennis parked me out here and served me some food, which I just finished eating." He sighed. "I was trying to rustle up enough energy to get back to my room."

"Do you want a hand?"

"I don't *want* a hand," he clarified, "but I think I might *need* a hand."

"And you know something? Just even understanding the difference is huge."

"After being in various stages of health over the years," Urban added, "I'm generally pretty good about asking for help."

"And if I weren't here right now, who would you ask?"

she asked curiously. "And you aren't preferring to stay in your room are you? Away from people? I notice you're out here alone."

"I probably would have asked Dennis about who I should call." His shoulders slumped.

"He would have just helped you back himself," she noted. As he shuffled in the chair, he winced. "The pain is bad again, isn't it? And I noticed you haven't answered my question."

"My back is always bad. And I've been sitting here too long, but the evening air was just so fresh and so welcoming," he shared, "that I didn't really want to go back to my room. And, no, I'm not trying to isolate myself. But being around people—new people—isn't the easiest. Being in a center like this is easier, as others have similar injuries, similar looks," he noted cautiously, "but there are a lot of normal people here, and I, … I stand out."

"It's hard to be new, but that will change quickly. And you don't stand out. Sure you're injured and scarred, but so is everyone here." She studied his face, the scars more noticeable, but now that she'd seen them, had become used to them, … well, he looked normal.

"If it wasn't quite so late, I'd take you out on a walk around the place," she said, "but I do have rounds, so can I help you back to your room?" He apparently took that as a sign that it was time to leave because he slowly pushed away from the table.

But she stepped up. "No, if there's a reason that you need help, then let me help."

He just sat back and waited for her to step around and to slowly maneuver the wheelchair around the table, then head toward the hallway. "From the looks of it," he stated,

"I'd say you've done this a time or two."

"Yeah, you think?" she quipped, laughing. "And that's okay. We'll all be doing it a time or two again and again and again. That's just part of life here."

"And you guys are okay with that?"

"Of course we are," she replied in surprise. "It is part of the work we do."

"I get that too," Urban agreed, "but it always just seems like it's more than what people really expect."

"I don't know about that," she said. "I think most people just don't know what life is fully about, not until they get into a scenario like this and are forced to deal with it. … The fact that you're totally okay to ask for help saves us a lot of trouble. And we don't want to make you feel worse. We just want to know that, when the time comes that you need help, that you will reach out and get it."

"I will," he declared. "You don't have to worry about that."

She chuckled. "I'm glad to hear it because people say that, but then they don't follow through."

"Isn't that the truth," he agreed, with a smile, "but that's not me."

"Good. In that case, let's get you back to your room." And they slowly wove around the dining room tables until they were heading in the right direction.

"I was getting tired just sitting out there. And I knew that, by the time I got myself back to my room, it would be more than I should be doing."

"Absolutely it would be," she confirmed. "And remember. That's why we're here."

He nodded. "But, at the same time, I just didn't want to admit that I was taking on too much," he admitted.

"Understood," she replied cheerfully. "And again, not a problem. Let's just get you safely back to your bed." And there, once in his room, she stopped, looked at him, and asked, "Do you need any more help from here?"

He shook his head. "I should be good. I'm not doing any more than brush my teeth and get myself into bed."

"Okay. I will go do a round of medications, and you'll be on that list," she shared. "I'll be back in say, fifteen to twenty." And, with that, she walked back out, but she was a little worried about the level of pain on his face that he wasn't doing very good at hiding. She made a note to check on him through the night to see if the pain was controlled enough.

When she returned with his pain meds, he reached for them a little too eagerly.

She nodded. "Now if this doesn't keep it under control for the night, you need to let me know," she said. "I don't want you suffering in silence. That won't help anything."

"I know," he noted, "and I'll try not to end up in that scenario, but ..." And he left it hanging.

"You *won't* because you'll let me know," she stated firm-ly.

"Yes, ma'am," he replied mockingly.

She shook her head at him. "Pain is not helpful. We get it. You don't like it. You don't like how some of the drugs probably make you feel. We can switch out your drugs. We can do all kinds of things. But being in constant pain won't get you better here."

He sighed, settled back into his bed, and whispered, "I know. ... I'd just like to sleep now."

She pulled the blanket atop him. "Then rest. Just rest." And, with that, he drifted off into sleep, even as she stayed at his side.

As soon as he looked to be out, the pain not jarring him awake, she headed off on the rest of her rounds.

URBAN WOKE UP the next morning feeling pretty decent. But he knew that that would flag quickly, once he was working with Shane. The warnings about him had been fully justified. And all Urban could do was try to keep things in control and to not let the pain get too far and too fast on him.

Even Shane told him, as Urban went through the next few days, "Remember. You must listen to your body. This isn't about what I want you to do. This isn't about what you want to do. It's about what your body needs you to do."

"And that sounds easy," Urban said, gasping for air as he collapsed onto the mat, a muscle cramp seizing him. "It's my back screaming at me always."

"Yep, I hear you." Shane quickly flipped him over and started to massage the area. By the time Urban groaned with relief, Shane pointed out, "We'll have to take your rehab back a step, let you slowly work up to it again."

"Everybody's taking it *slowly*," Urban complained, "and the net effect is, it's not improving."

"It will improve," Shane declared, "but we must deal with a lot of muscles here and there first."

Urban wasn't even sure what all that meant. And it would be days before he fully understood.

And by the time he rolled into Shane's gym a week later, Shane looked up, smiling, then frowned. "Oh, I don't think I like the look on your face right now."

"It's not so much a look. I just know that your sessions tend to be hard," Urban admitted.

"Are they too hard though?" Shane asked, looking at him intently.

"I don't think so. I'm trying to listen to my body, but it's not all that easy."

"No, it isn't, but, as long as you're trying, then your body will try back."

"It's definitely working on it," he noted, with a tense smile. "It's just that I've had easier jobs in my life."

"Yep, I get it. Now, if you're ready, let's get to work."

And Urban didn't know whether things were getting better, easier, or Shane had just taken it down a notch on him today. When he was done and slowly working his way back into his wheelchair, Urban asked, "Was that an easier session today?"

"No," he confirmed. "Yet, bit by bit, your back is slowly strengthening."

"You think so?" Urban asked hopefully, as Shane smiled at him.

Shane nodded. "I know so. We'll keep on going this way for a bit." He looked at his watch and asked, "How do you feel about doing a few finishing exercises in the hot tub?"

"In the hot tub might not be too bad," Urban clarified, "but I am pretty exhausted though."

"And that's one of the reasons for the hot tub. You told me that you were doing better today." Shane studied him.

"I am, but I'm still tired. Even a half session with you is way more work than I've done in a very long time."

"And yet you were in rehab before." Shane shook his head. "So I don't understand that."

"It was different. The work was different. The people

were different. The push was different," he replied. "I would hate to think that I wasn't working as hard back then because I certainly thought I was. However, it wasn't leaving me quite so exhausted all the time, like here."

"And I don't want you *exhausted*-exhausted," Shane pointed out, "but I definitely don't want you so comfortable that you don't push it. When you told me that today was easier, I just thought that maybe you would like to do some more in the hot tub."

"I would like to do the hot tub, yes," he said. "Let's see how it works."

"Good. Hopefully it won't be too bad." And, with that, they arranged to meet at the hot tub within twenty minutes.

"You know how to get there?" Shane asked.

"I've only seen it from over the deck," Urban replied. "I presume there's an elevator or some way to get down there." When Shane gave him the directions to the elevator, Urban remembered seeing it.

"Good enough," Urban said. "I can try that." Getting changed and getting down there, however, was a whole different story. By the time he was on his way to the elevator, he was sorry he had agreed to this. Why did just getting changed after a rehab session exhaust him so much? It made no sense. And yet that's the way he always felt after one with Shane. When the elevator opened, he was surprised to see chaos reigning. He stared in astonishment as a man raced down the hallway, two women at his side, and puppies bouncing down the hall, trying to avoid capture.

Urban wanted to laugh, but, at the same time, he knew that nobody would appreciate it. But neither would he stop and roll past this spectacle. When the man managed to scoop up one and then another puppy, they started shrieking in the most horrible manner. Urban could tell that they weren't hurt; obviously it was more fear than anything.

Then the puppies calmed down almost immediately when the man spoke to them.

Urban stared, astonished.

At that, the man turned and walked toward where Urban sat in his chair. "That must have looked like fun, *huh?*"

"I'm not so sure about the fun part, other than for the puppies," Urban noted, shaking his head. "I do remember talk from other people about animals," he said hesitantly, "but I'm not exactly sure why animals are here."

The man reached out a hand and said, "I'm Stan. Most of the people who come here already know about my veterinarian clinic, which occupies the lowest floor of Hathaway House."

Urban shook his head. "No, I didn't know anything about it. Seriously?"

Stan pointed to the offices behind him. "Yep. Anytime you want to come visit with the animals, come see us. We're all part of the same center, in a way. I just look after animal patients."

Astonished, Urban watched as the two women, big grins on their faces, walked past him carrying the other puppies. "I'm not sure what the deal is with the puppies, but any chance I could hold one for a sec?"

Stan stepped back and let the ladies go through to the other room, while Stan dropped a puppy onto Urban's lap. "Anytime you want more of this kind of canine love, I've always got pets around here," Stan offered. "We also have a mammoth rabbit and various other animals, and we work with a lot of therapy animals too. So, you'll see them visiting patients upstairs as well."

"I haven't been blessed enough to see that yet," Urban murmured, as he hugged the puppy, "but I am definitely interested." And the puppy, as if realizing that he was safe and would get cuddles and love, immediately started wiggling in his arms and jumping up to lick his face.

"You have to love animals to be here," Stan declared, as he stood nearby, the other puppy in his arms wiggling to get out.

"I do," he murmured. "I just had no idea that this was down here."

"If you're new, it takes a bit to even understand what's going on with the process upstairs, and, of course, not everybody passes on information about our floor because so many people already know."

"And I wasn't planning to even come here to Hathaway House," he shared. "I had another center I was supposed to go to, and then that got canceled, and I ended up here."

"That," the vet declared, raising his eyebrows, "is a very lucky break for you."

"So I've been told." Urban laughed. "And the fact that you have the animals is, … is huge."

"It is, indeed, and we thoroughly enjoy our escapades with them, but not when somebody, one of our clients, accidentally leaves the door open, while we're giving the puppies some exercise."

"Nope, I can see that." Urban smiled. Reluctantly he handed the puppy back. "I'm due at the hot tub, so I'd better get going."

Stan scooped up the puppy and held him close to his chest and then added, "Anytime you want to visit, just make your way through those double doors there. The clinic is always open to animal lovers. And we always have animals that need a hug or a cuddle," he noted. "They need it as much as people do."

"Got it." Urban was fascinated, as Stan disappeared down the hallway. Urban slowly turned his wheelchair in the direction of the double exit doors in front of him and hit the big button to open up the door, so he could get out.

As he appeared, Shane looked over at him and nodded. "I was afraid I would have to send a search party."

"For future reference," Urban replied, "the first place you need to look is the vet clinic." He motioned back there. "A bunch of puppies escaped, right when I came out of the elevator. They were trying to round them up."

At that, Shane laughed. "We've lost more than a few people to Stan's clinic." Shane smiled. "The patients here love going down there."

"I didn't even know it was here, but now that I do …" Urban beamed.

"Now that you do, you can be a regular visitor and enjoy all the puppy love you want. We also have several therapy cats and therapy dogs as part of our rehab program. I'm surprised you haven't seen them yet."

"No, I haven't, and maybe I've just been so focused on getting to where I need to be on time and taking care of all the rest of the things in my life that I didn't even notice them," he murmured, thinking of the number of hours he'd stayed in his room. Animals were pure joy. They never judged by appearance. Still, to be honest, he hadn't had the same judgmental or intrusive looks from anyone here. A couple of the patients had asked him what had happened, commiserating over their shared wounds, but, other than that, everyone had treated Urban the same—normal.

Coming back to Shane's comment, Urban added,

"Maybe I thought they were visitors." He shook his head. "Either way, I have to admit it was quite fun to see the puppies today."

"It always is." Shane flashed a bright smile. "They can have a huge impact on people and individual healing."

"I can imagine," he murmured. "My heart goes out to the poor animals in situations that they end up here."

"And keep that thought," Shane said, "because that's how most of us feel about you guys. We would do anything to make your lives a little easier and to get you a little further down the healing pathway, so that you can have the kind of life that you want."

Shane motioned at the building around them. "We can't replace legs and muscle and bones here, but we can make what you have do so much more for you. We just need your cooperation—your *assistance*, I guess, is a better word—and we will all work together to make it happen." And, with that, he pointed to the hot tub. "Let's get you in there, where we can soak some of those muscles, and then we can start doing some stretches on your back. I want to see just how much range of movement you have."

"As long as you won't try to get me into any pretzel shapes," he joked.

Shane gave him a knowing look. "We just hired somebody new to run a Pilates and yoga program. Don't kid yourself. The minute you can do most of those movements, you won't need us anymore."

"My body does not bend that way."

"Let's see how far we can get it to go."

"If you say so," Urban muttered. And, with that, he made his way awkwardly and painfully to the hot tub.

"I guess walking would be one of the first priorities in

your world, wouldn't it?"

"Absolutely," Urban said.

"You're not far away from it though," Shane noted.

"I'm *too* far away from it," Urban argued, with a head-shake. "What cup are you drinking from that you see anything different?"

Shane burst out laughing. "The cup of truth. I get it. You're not mentally there yet, but really, once we get your back and core strengthened," Shane explained, "we'll get those legs to do what we need them to do."

Urban stared at him in astonishment. Yet that breath of hope broke through his heart. "I sure hope you're right," he said almost painfully, as he slithered on his butt the last little bit to the hot tub and slipped his legs over the side. "It sure doesn't seem like that to me."

"Nope, it never does when it's you in that situation. Never fear. I've seen it before. Not injuries exactly like this of course," he added, "but I have seen lots of people who have thought they would never walk again. My deal is to ensure that you do." And, with that, he motioned at the water. "Now let's start by floating first, so that we can heat up all those muscles, and then we'll do a bunch of stretches."

At that, Urban slipped all the way into the water and just floated in the middle. "If you'd told me that we could just come down here and float, I wouldn't have argued."

Shane chuckled. "Floating warms up the muscles and lets your spine straighten out, without the resistance and the weight of gravity," he explained. "So we'll do a bunch of the exercises while you're literally prone like that. After this, make sure you put cream on the burn tissue, so that it doesn't get irritated from the chemicals in the hot tub. It will help keep the skin moist and supple too."

Urban smiled over at him. "Good thing Bettina gave me some then, isn't it?"

"It is." Shane returned a smile. "But not to worry. Even if you didn't have some already, I would find you some."

Urban laughed at that. "I guess you don't let anybody off the hook, do you?"

"Letting you off the hook isn't doing you a favor," Shane noted, "and it won't get us to where we need to go, so no. The only time you're off the hook is when your body says we're done."

"And that'll happen before I tell you that I'm done," Urban admitted. "So let's get started."

Chapter 5

BETTINA POPPED IN and checked on Urban several times over the next few days. She managed to keep the conversations light, but, with an assessing gaze, checked how he was doing. A lot of people reacted very differently when Shane got them to start moving. Some rejected all that he had to offer. Some dove in with both feet and some took it cautiously, afraid of the pain heading their way. In Urban's case she wasn't sure yet. He seemed to be taking it cautiously but was fairly surefooted.

When she brought it up with Shane a few days later, he nodded. "Urban's handling it pretty well. The only thing is, I'm afraid he's not listening to his body."

"That's an interesting comment," she murmured, "because a lot of them don't—or at least not until it's too late."

"And a lot of them don't realize what they have to listen to," Shane noted. "That's another problem all in itself. Just because they're listening doesn't mean they're actually hearing."

She chuckled. "And who knew that having so many physical issues could make that whole conversation so difficult."

"But it is, for even you and me," Shane explained. "If I were to ask you to go on a 10K run, what would your body say?"

"Heck no," she replied instantly.

He chuckled. "And yet, for a lot of people, they'd be up and raring to go. And maybe not even listening to what their body would say. Their mind would say yes, but their body may say something completely different."

"Ah, right. Got it. My mind is, like, *Absolutely no way*, and my body is sitting here complacently agreeing. *Yep, she's got that right.*"

He grinned at her. "But you're not a runner, and, if you were a runner before you had an injury, you could be itching to get back to it."

"Yeah, I'm not a runner, never was a runner, can't imagine anybody itching to get back to it," she stated, with a shudder.

"But for those who *are* runners," Shane pointed out, "not being able to feel the wind on their face and the earth under their feet and that power move through their body is hard. They don't get that high euphoric feeling unless they are running. They don't get that same rush anymore. And, if you're completely set back in life right now, like somebody with these major injuries, there's no rush at all, there's no adrenaline high out of life. Is that why people run? That's why a lot of people run. It gives them a sense of exhilaration and a sense of being one with the world, feeling their body churn mile after mile after mile and feeling that distance in their headspace. It almost, for some of them, gives them a chance to just disconnect from the world around them."

Bettina frowned. "I've never had that kind of an experience, but I'm not a runner. … It's never been my thing."

"And, therefore, to you, that doesn't matter in the least, but, for some of these guys, it matters a lot."

"More to learn and to understand," she admitted, with a

bright smile.

"Yeah, for all of us," Shane agreed. "I'm not much of a runner, but I do know many have come through this place, and what they really wanted to get back was that ability. Depending on their injuries, they may or may not. For some guys who lost their legs, it's pretty traumatizing. Some of them go on to run, even with prosthetics. It depends on how much it matters to you and what you were getting out of it and what you're hoping to get out of it now."

"And I don't know all that much about Urban yet," Bettina said. "I do try to get to know everybody here, but, so far, something's almost defeating about him. I don't know." She stopped, thought about it, and added, "As if a soldier, waiting for the wrong answer, expecting to do the work regardless, but not getting the payout."

"In a way, maybe," Shane agreed cautiously. "However, I don't think he's defeated at all—which is a good thing—and he's here, yet he didn't know that he was supposed to come here. It was one of those very strange mix-ups, and somehow he's here regardless. And I don't think he realizes how lucky he is."

"No, he doesn't," she replied. "I mean, we all believe in what we do here, but Urban doesn't know very much about it, so, for him, this is a strange shift in his world."

"He'll get used to it pretty fast," Shane noted cheerfully. "In the meantime, if you see anything odd or anything that needs to be brought up, let me know."

"Will do." And Bettina watched as Shane headed down the hallway. Urban had come a long way, but there was still a distancing within himself, as if he were afraid of getting hurt or getting the short stick again. She wanted to bring it up with him but didn't dare. She wasn't a shrink, and that wasn't part of her job in any way. Still, at the same time, she did wonder how he was making out.

When she arrived at work a bit early for her shift, on impulse she picked up two coffees and headed to Urban's room. It was foolish because, well, he could have been at the pool or still sleeping or even at Stan's. She didn't know where he was. She hadn't checked in to even see if he wanted a coffee. His door was closed when she got there. Frowning, she wondered if she should knock.

One of the orderlies came by, and, holding up the two cups of coffee, she asked, "Could you knock on that door for me?"

When a shout to come in followed, the orderly opened the door for her. She stepped inside and said, "Hey. Now I didn't even think about it, but I automatically stopped and picked you up a coffee."

A pleased grin crossed his face. "I won't say no, and I am definitely surprised, but it's a good surprise."

"Good," she replied sheepishly. "I don't want you to think that I'm bothering you."

"You can bother me all you want," he stated, "particularly if you do it with coffee."

At that, she burst out laughing. "That's good to know, … although I still feel as if I'm making a nuisance of myself." He rolled his eyes at that, but she shrugged. "When I automatically pick up a coffee for someone, without forethought, it makes me wonder why."

"You did it because you absolutely knew I needed one," he suggested.

And then she noted that he appeared to be freshly showered and that his hair was wet. "Shower or pool?" she asked.

"Both. First one, then the other."

"And it's early in the day for you to be done with rehab."

"Yeah, I'm the one who called it quits today," he admitted. "I'm dealing with the guilt of that."

"I wouldn't," she argued. "If you're feeling as if you needed to call it quits, then you call it quits."

"Yeah, but you also know that it feels like being a quitter, and, in my world, you don't do that. When we have to pass some of our exams to do what we do," he explained, "there's just no quitting. It's … It's like the worst thing you can do. It's also why very few of us made the grade."

She stared at him for a long moment. "Don't suppose you were a SEAL, were you?" He nodded slowly. "Of course. So quitting, for you, is the opposite of what you've been trained to do."

"Exactly. At the same time, I also know that hurting my body won't help me to heal as fast either."

"So maybe you shouldn't think of it as quitting," she suggested, "but maybe as a timeout."

"Still sounds like quitting to me," he confirmed in a droll tone.

She smiled. "That's just a mind-set."

"Maybe, but it's the one that I'm working with, and it's not the easiest."

"No, I can't imagine that it would be." And she knew very much about the BUD/S training and what the men went through from other patients who had been here at Hathaway House. Thus she had a pretty good idea how much of a struggle this would be for him. "When you do your military training, is it ever brought up about quitting when your body needs to quit?" He just looked at her, his eyebrows raised, and she nodded. "No, of course not. It's *go until you drop*, isn't it?"

"Kinda," he agreed cheerfully. "And, once you're in that mind-set, it's really hard to shift."

"I get that, but aren't you no longer in that mind-set?"

"No, not at the moment, but that doesn't mean that I can just drop it."

"Even after all the surgeries and all the work that you've done to get here?"

"No." He placed his coffee down and smiled, just as she turned and headed away. "Hey, you have to leave?" he protested.

She looked at her watch and shrugged. "I got a couple minutes."

"Good. Take a seat." And he pointed to the visitor's chair.

"Haven't you had enough to do with people yet today?" she joked.

"Yeah, especially people who are pushing and prodding and making me do stuff I don't want to do," he stated, with a bright grin. "But for a beautiful woman who delivers coffee? No."

She flushed at that. "You're just a smooth talker," she quipped, with a bright smile.

"Hey, it's appreciated no matter what. If my flirting skills are a little rusty," Urban said, "I definitely appreciate the coffee. I am tired. I was in the pool working, and then I came back and had a shower but ..."

She nodded. "It's all about listening to your body."

"We're back to that again, *huh*?"

"We have to be, in a way," she shared, "but I don't have to hound you about it."

He burst out laughing. "I think hounding is something you all do anyway."

She winced. "Are we that bad?"

He shrugged. "Maybe not all the time, but it seems as if we always have something to be working on."

"Everyone—even I have to be working on something." He stopped and stared, and she shrugged. "Sometimes there's just family stuff you must deal with, whether you want to or not."

"Tell me about your family," he urged her.

She laughed. "Not a whole lot to tell. There's just my brother and me and my mom, but she remarried and is living back East."

"Wow. Do you see her much?"

"Nope, I don't see her at all."

"And is that by choice?"

"Yeah, sure is. I don't like her new partner."

"Ah, that's too bad."

"Maybe, and maybe it's for the best."

"It's kind of sad. If that's the case, I'm sure she didn't marry to get away from you."

"No, but she also married because she couldn't stand on her own two feet." Bettina flushed at that. "I didn't mean for that to sound quite so harsh."

"No, but it's an honest opinion on your part," Urban noted. "And I've certainly known several women who felt they couldn't live without a male partner."

"Yeah, that's my mom." Bettina shrugged. "I'm not of the same mind-set. I'd rather find somebody who is like me and who wants to do the same things, like me, instead of making my world like the other person's."

"I think it should be a compromise, but what do I know? I've never been married."

"Not even close?" she asked.

"No, not in the field I was in. It always seemed like I would be leaving her to deal with that pain of separation all the time and that fear about my safety, and I didn't want that for anybody. Now, of course …" Almost subconsciously he reached up and massaged the tight skin on his neck.

"But it's not the same situation now," she murmured. "And you're still young, vibrant, and a hero, so I'm sure a lot of interested women are out there looking for you."

He shot her a look of disbelief. "I'm not sure what you're drinking, but there isn't exactly a big market for broken-down men."

She stared at him. "No, there isn't, but there *is* a big market for men who have been through the wringer and have come out the other side, all the better for it. And the scars on your face are minor. Barely noticeable after the first glance." There was such shock in his gaze that she nodded. "Yes, I mean it. The scars are minor."

He stared at her. "I don't know if I qualify yet, as I haven't gotten to the other side of this mess," he began, "but, if you know of an online dating app that's got something like that, let me know."

She heard the humor in his tone and smirked. "I'm serious. No, I don't think there is a dating app or a dating site for that," she replied, "but it takes a lot for some people to grow up—like, really grow up and understand what life is all about. And to see the real person under the injuries?" Her voice was gentle, as she added, "Most of the people we find here have already grown up the hard way, through trial and sometimes defeat and sometimes pain, sometimes massive injuries. Very few people who come in here with major injuries haven't also lost friends or had some badly injured. And so much more. What about you? Who do you have for family?"

"Two brothers," Urban shared, "one still in the military and one in business."

"Ah. So that's good. Maybe you could work with your civilian brother."

He frowned at her. "I hadn't thought about it," he murmured. "It might be worth approaching him."

"Does he know where you are?"

"No, not right now," he said, with a laugh. "With my transfer, everything happened so fast that I didn't really get a chance to let people in on my change of residence."

"Then you might want to," she suggested, with a smile. "He could be freaking out, looking for you."

"I don't know." Urban frowned. "He's not the kind to freak."

"Maybe not, but that doesn't mean he isn't the kind to care."

Urban tilted his head at that, picked up his coffee, and took a healthy sip, and then he settled back. "It's really good coffee."

She chuckled. "That's just because you like the delivery person."

"Oh, I really like her," he agreed, with a bright smile.

She laughed, looked at her watch, and added, "I unfortunately have to go."

"Good enough," he replied. "Stop by when you get a moment, if you just want to talk and visit."

"Yeah, wouldn't that be nice," she said. "The way the system works is, when I get a chance to talk and visit, everybody else is asleep."

"I'm not always asleep," he pointed out. "Too often I'm wide awake at nighttime."

She frowned, as she studied him. "Do you want something to help you with that?"

He shook his head. "I prefer to be as drug-free as possible. It just eats away in my brain if I get too much in there."

"As long as you're not worrying about something," she scolded lightly.

"I wouldn't dare around this place," he admitted. "You would put it all on my list of things to work on."

At that, she burst out laughing, walked to the door, and nodded. "Now that I sat here and drank all my coffee with you, I have to go get another one. … Do you need more?"

He shook his head. "No, I'm good now. Thanks."

And she headed out.

URBAN NOTED SOMETHING was just inherently nice about that woman. The fact that Bettina was also a looker didn't hurt in the least. Neither did the fact that she didn't appear to be bothered by his facial scars. She was special in a way that he hadn't expected to find anybody special in a very long time. And maybe because she worked at a place like this, but she didn't even seem to really notice or care about his injuries, but then again it's not as if they were talking on a romantic level.

He could hope for something like that, but he was a long way from it. He really did wish for a database for broken-down people to find others, but then he was not in an easy physical or mental state to match up quite yet either. Still, he would continue to work on his healing as he always did, and hopefully the rest of his life would fill in a little more easily for him. But today Shane had put Urban through the workout pretty heavily, and he was on the tired side as it was. He settled in his bed, when his phone rang.

"Where are you?" David asked.

Urban laughed. "Somebody just reminded me that I hadn't updated people on my change of residence."

"I stopped in the hospital," David declared, "and you weren't even there. What happened?" His voice rose in anger.

"Sorry if I wasted your time."

"Hey, it's not that you wasted my time. I was worried."

"*Right.*" Urban groaned. "Seriously I have just been overwhelmed at this new location, and, well, I've just never even thought of it."

"You need to think of it a little more often," he stated. "You aren't alone in this world, and we do care about what happens. Where are you?"

"I'm at Hathaway House."

"Hathaway House." He rolled it around in his brain. "Good Lord, that's where Shane works."

"You know Shane?"

"Yeah, have you met him yet?"

"Yeah," Urban muttered on a dry note. "I see him every day."

David started to laugh. "Is he working with you?"

"He's working *me*. I don't know if there's a *with me* in a part of that or not," he quipped, with a note of humor.

"You know that he's been up for all kinds of awards and honors," David shared. "That guy is supposed to be the best there is."

"Really?" Urban asked.

"Yeah, how have you found him so far?"

"Fair but tough," he murmured.

"That should suit you to a tee then. That's definitely all about your world, isn't it?"

"Maybe," he conceded. "I hadn't really expected to see it here."

"And maybe they're doing it specifically because it is what you are used to," David noted calmly. "So, you're not all that far away from me."

"Maybe not."

"Are you okay if I come down for a visit?"

"Sure am," Urban agreed. "How's business?"

"That's one of the things I want to talk to you about. I won't make it tonight," he said. "Maybe tomorrow?"

"Sure. After my workday would be good."

"Hey, you're talking to someone who doesn't even know what the meaning of a normal *workday* is," David stated. "You tell me what time to show up, and I'll be there." So they made arrangements for 4:30 p.m. the next day.

And, with that, Urban smiled as he hung up the phone. "I hadn't expected that to happen," he murmured.

But he was looking forward to it. David was the one brother Urban had always gotten along with, mostly because David had fully supported Urban's choice to go into the military. And, in return, Urban had fully supported David's choice to go into business after leaving the military. Their father hadn't supported either of them. He had a career working for the government in accounting, which was something none of the sons wanted. Still their father had hoped that somebody would follow in his footsteps, but Urban knew it wouldn't happen in this lifetime. At least not in this generation, maybe later but not now.

So Urban hadn't spent any time talking to his father in the ensuing years. And maybe that was too bad. Urban considered giving him a call, but then realized he could only handle so much at once, and David would be more than enough. Urban rarely talked to Danny, his eldest brother and usually only when there was an opportunity, or something was coming down the military pipeline that he should know about.

Of course now that Urban had been injured and discharged from the navy, everything along that military line ever after had come to a stop. So Danny knew that Urban was in a rehab center somewhere, but he didn't know anything about Urban's condition. Urban wondered if he should send Danny a message.

If David knew about Hathaway House, surely Danny did too. Urban frowned, picked up his phone, and texted Danny, letting his eldest brother know where he was. When a **Wow** text came back almost immediately, Urban wondered what that meant. His phone rang a few minutes later.

"Not sure how you made that happen," Danny began, "but you are blessed."

"Because I'm here?"

"Yep," he said. "That place is really starting to get a rep, and, if I were ever injured, you can bet that's where I would be."

"*If* they had room for you, you would be," Urban pointed out, chuckling.

"I don't know how you got in."

"I'm not exactly sure either. I was supposed to go somewhere else, but this is where I ended up."

"Lucky you," Danny said. "You have a chance to rebuild your life at that place."

"That's what I'm hoping," Urban stated, surprised at everybody's response. "I honestly didn't know anything about this place."

"Even more astonishing because the waitlist is quite something apparently."

Urban hadn't even considered that, but obviously somebody was looking out for him, and he was grateful.

"Any chance of you getting back on your feet anytime soon?" Danny asked.

"According to Shane there is."

"I would trust them. They've seen every kind of injury possible coming out of our lovely military," he noted.

For the first time, Urban recognized almost a weariness in his brother's voice. "You okay?"

"Yeah, … I just lost a buddy here two days ago. I'm still feeling the effects of that."

Urban cursed. "I'm sorry. I don't think there's anything worse."

"Yeah, there is something worse," Danny declared. "Finding out your brother is badly injured—but at least you didn't die."

"Nope, I didn't die. And I'm struggling with all kinds of injuries, but I'm getting there."

"And I'm really glad to hear that," Danny replied sincerely. "Have you talked to Dad?"

"No, I haven't. I've kind of avoided it."

"Yeah, me too," Danny admitted. "He didn't really like any of our career choices, and I'm sure he'd not be terribly happy about where you are right now."

"No, and I don't want to listen to *I told you so* either."

At that, Danny burst out laughing. "Yeah, isn't that the truth," he murmured. "Still, you sound better than I had thought to hear from you."

"Because I'm not in my usual place, as David would put

it, I sent that text. I realized I hadn't updated him either."

"And you're still close to him?"

"Yeah, he's coming here tomorrow."

"Good," Danny replied. "Say hi to him for me."

"I will." In the background he heard Danny being called.

"I have to go."

"I know you do."

And, with that, his eldest brother rang off.

Urban stared at the phone, realizing how foreign that military world was again, how different it sounded to not be a part of military life, and yet to hear it going on in the background. It was hard to acknowledge that that part of Urban's life was over. It's all he'd ever wanted really, and, once you've got your sights hooked on to something like that, it was hard to see anything else in your life. Maybe that had been part of the problem, when Urban had chosen that direction. He'd just kept on going, one foot in front of the other, never really considering any other options.

And now look at him. He had no other options, as far as he knew, and that's where the problems were coming from. What would he do with his life from here on out? He could only hope that maybe, as he spent time here, something would shake loose as far as ideas, and he would come up with some plan for his life that would make him feel better. And, with that, he closed his eyes and had a nap.

Chapter 6

THE EVENING WAS busy, and Bettina never got a chance to stop in and see Urban again. When a man stopped her in the hallway the next day, asking for Urban's room, she smiled up at him. "You must be his brother."

He looked at her in surprise and asked, "Does he tell people I'm coming?"

"Maybe just me," she replied, with a shrug, "but come on. I'll show you his room." And she led him down the hallway to where she suspected Urban would be waiting. When she knocked on the door, there was no answer. She opened it, peeked inside, and smiled. "Hey."

He looked up and said, "Hey."

"Your brother's here," she murmured.

He looked at her in surprise, and she opened the door wider for the visitor to step through. At that, the two men embraced.

Tears filled her eyes at the obvious affection between them. She quickly stepped back and away and left them. She had plenty of work to keep her busy but could only hope that the two men had things to work out or at least maybe just needed time together.

Meanwhile, some people had no visitors and suffered because they didn't have any living relatives. Thus seeing other people get visitors reminded them that they had none.

Bettina took special care with those lonely souls, and that's how her day went—some crying out because they didn't have any visitors. Even people with family still didn't have anybody who visited either because of time and distance or money or demanding jobs.

People needed people.

THE NEXT DAY for Bettina rolled around, which meant her night shift was about to start. By the time she headed to get some dinner, she saw Urban on the deck, talking intently to someone. She wasn't so sure what that was all about but, hey, it looked positive, and she was more than happy for him. She ate her meal with a couple nurses, ready to start her shift. As she headed out, Urban called out to her.

"Hey, Bettina."

She turned, and he motioned her over. She realized his brother was visiting again. She smiled at him. "Glad to see you again."

David smiled. "Have you worked here long?" he asked her.

"Yep, quite a few years now," she shared. "It's an amazing place to be."

"It's got an unbelievable rep." Just then he looked behind her, and his grin widened. He hopped to his feet and cried out, "Shane."

At that, she turned to watch Shane take one look at the visitor and come bolting over. The two men hugged and slapped each other on the back, before Shane stepped back and asked, "What are you doing here?"

"I don't know how it happened," David began, "but this

is my brother." And he pointed at Urban.

Shane looked at Urban, back at David, and frowned. "Really?"

David nodded. "Yeah, really. So you have to treat my brother right."

"I treat everybody right," Shane stated, laughing. He looked over at Urban. "You didn't tell me that this was your brother."

"I didn't know you knew him. Plus I wasn't sure if he would show up again today."

At that, David groaned. "When you don't show for *one* appointment outta your life, *that's* the one thing that they bring up every day, ever after."

Shane grinned. "Isn't that the truth. Hey, look. I'm grabbing some dinner. Do you mind if I sit with you?"

"No, come on. Come on," David replied. "I didn't even think that I would have a chance to see you during this visit."

"I'm just glad you came," Shane added. "One of the things about this place that we really try to encourage, but it doesn't always happen, is to have visitors. Yet some people don't have anybody." He pointed to the buffet line and took off.

At that, David sighed. "Urban's got me and our eldest brother, but our father won't come. It would be … I don't know that he could handle it."

"And maybe you would surprise yourself," Bettina added. "Injuries like this tend to change a person."

"They do, indeed," Urban replied, "and it just reminds him that he told all of us *not* to go into the military."

She smiled, patted Urban's shoulder, and announced, "I can't stay. I'm due on shift, but it was nice meeting you,

David." And she took off.

AT THAT, DAVID looked over at his brother. "A special friend?"

Urban flushed. He wished. "Let's just say a friend. I'm not sure how anything in my condition can be made *special*. Especially this face."

"I wouldn't knock it, and she doesn't seem to be bothered by it all," David said, "but it is not an easy world out there."

"Yeah? How's Marion doing?"

"She broke off with me," he replied starkly. "Didn't like that I was a workaholic, and—according to her—didn't like that I didn't pay enough attention to her, and it just goes on and on and on."

"And is she right?"

"Probably," David admitted, "but it's enough to make me stop and realize *why* I was working too much—in order to *not* have much time with her. We've also been fighting over money. She spends at a rate that I just … I can't even begin to keep up with," he shared, "and it's fairly distressing to me."

"Of course and you don't spend at all."

"With her around, it was almost instinctive to put the brakes on her. I mean, she would spend her evenings shopping. We wouldn't go to a movie. The outing was only about shopping. Then she started buying online. I've never seen anything like it. It did have me concerned."

"Sounds like maybe the two of you weren't all that suited."

"Maybe. But it's hard because, well, you invest a lot of your life with a certain person, and then, all of a sudden, they decide that you're not right."

"And how much of that is just an ego trip, and you're more hurt than anything?"

"I don't know," David said. "I really don't know."

"And is there a particular reason to come here?"

His brother looked at him oddly. "No. Not necessarily."

"Which just makes me even more suspicious," Urban noted, looking at him. "Before Shane gets here, you want to tell me?"

David sighed. "I don't know what you'll do when you're done here," he began, "but I wondered if you want to go into business with me."

"You know that I don't know anything about your businesses." Urban frowned at his brother.

"You don't know anything about the business side of them, but you were always very good at meeting core business needs. You were the one who started the lemonade stand. You were the one doing the golf ball collecting out of the ponds and selling them back to the guys. You were always very entrepreneurial."

Urban stared at his brother for a long moment and nodded. "I forgot all about that." And he started to chuckle.

"Yeah. That's what I mean. You've always been at the heart of it all."

"Yes, but it's your businesses."

"And I was wondering about doing a couple other businesses too." David studied his brother. "I don't want to make you feel bad, but I just don't know what your capabilities are."

"Neither do I," Urban stated just as bluntly as his brother. "But, according to Shane, there won't be a whole lot I can't do."

At that, Shane rejoined then, his dinner in tow, saying, "And that's right. By the time we're done with you here at Hathaway House, you should be doing pretty well."

"So walking?" David asked.

"Yes." Shane nodded. "Maybe not long 10K hikes to start with, but definitely walking."

"Sitting for long periods of time? Better to be standing if that's the case," Urban murmured.

"Nobody should be sitting for long periods of time, even you," Shane declared, turning to David.

David just smiled at that.

"He's wondering if I want to go into business with him," Urban stated. "He's worried about my future."

"Glad somebody is," Shane quipped.

David added, "The world's full of opportunities out there. If you have something to offer, go for it."

"That's the trouble," Urban said. "I don't know that I have anything to offer. I don't really want a pity job. On the other hand, … if it's no job versus a pity job, I'll take a pity job."

His brother burst out laughing, but that was the end of the business talk for now, instead catching up with Shane and letting him finish his dinner.

Shane stood. "Good to see you, David. Hope to see you again when you're here next." And he left the two brothers alone.

"You know, that comment about the pity job, coming from anybody else," David began, "I would be insulted. But, in your case, I know where this is coming from. It's definitely a real job. And I'm hoping it would be a case of being partners, not a job."

Urban stared at him. "You're serious about those new businesses, aren't you?"

"I definitely am. A big wide world is out there, and a big market to pick up on." David smiled. "I'm not so sure that I want to do *all* of it, all at once, *but,* if I had somebody else on board to bounce ideas off of and to see what we can do together," David suggested, "it might be fun."

"Anything in particular?"

"All kinds of them," David said, "from digital to opening a gym."

"Opening a gym?" Urban stared at him.

"Yeah. And, depending on what kind of condition you're in," David added, "it *was* a dream that you always wanted to have of your own."

"You mean, before I became hamburger?"

"Or if you don't *stay hamburger*," David corrected, "maybe it's something you would want to have again."

Urban sat back and stared. "And how's your financial situation?"

David flushed. "Mine's fine, … particularly with my fiancée no longer involved. She was spending money at an incredible rate."

"Seriously?"

"Oh, yeah, seriously. Like ten grand a month on her credit cards."

"So who's paying for it now?"

"Presumably she is," David replied, with a laugh, "but I really don't know. However, I'm not paying them anymore. I was paying, but I told her, *No more,* and that's probably why she broke up with me. I made it pretty clear I would not pay for this any longer."

"No, of course not," Urban agreed. "Debts like that aren't terribly normal. Maybe if she were buying or refurbishing a house …"

"It wasn't that for sure. It was spas and ladies' nights out and shopping for new outfits, even though she had a closet full." He shook his head. "I get it. It's her prerogative, *if* she's paying, and now she is. So she can do what she wants, but for me? It was … It was tough to watch it all happen."

"It doesn't sound as if you guys were in any way on the same page," Urban pointed out.

"You could be right." David nodded, with a brief chuckle. "And honestly, since we split up, I feel more than relieved."

After a few minutes of silence, as they both contemplated life and where they were at—whether they had expected to be here or not—his brother then piped up. "And don't forget. I've been investing that money you got from Grandpa."

Urban stared at him. "I completely forgot about that."

"I figured you probably had," David said, "but you're not destitute. I know you'll get your pension too—whatever that amounts to."

His brother's tone made it clear that David didn't think Urban's pension would be very much. "No, I won't be destitute," Urban declared, "but I do need to find something to do with my life. … I've been contemplating options but hadn't really come up with anything."

"If you come into business with me," David pointed out, "I can take more time off."

Urban laughed. "So are you trying to convince me to come for my sake or to come for your sake?"

"Either. Both." David smirked. "If you help prevent me

from overworking," he explained, "that would be a good thing too."

"You really haven't learned how to rest, have you?"

"Have you?" his brother challenged.

Urban snorted. "No, I'm still not very good at that myself."

"So maybe we can learn together," David suggested, with a smile.

"That would be kind of nice," Urban admitted. "We've always worked well together."

"It's one of the reasons why I was thinking of it," David shared. "We've always been able to talk. We've always been able to communicate. Now, if it involved our eldest brother, maybe not so much."

Urban nodded. "Yeah, I hear you there. As it is, we probably could do this." He added, "I just don't know what kind of business I would want to get into."

"And that's a fair enough question too," David noted. "We have time to consider our options. All kinds of business opportunities are out there." He pointed to his briefcase. "I brought a folder. A bunch of paperwork for you to consider."

"Really?" Urban asked, a bit shocked. "Were you that sure?"

"No, in your case I'm never sure," he stated, with a smile. "You do have a tendency to go off and to do things in your own world."

"I do that," Urban confirmed. "Still, maybe it's not so far out of the realm of possibility for us to do this together."

"I think we can," David murmured. "I don't know what you are looking for. Maybe you want something different for your life now."

"I'll have to see," he said. "I'm not exactly sure myself."

At that, David hopped up, pulled the big folder from his briefcase, and passed it to Urban. "I've got to go. Let me know if you have any thoughts about this."

"Will do." Urban smiled at his brother, as he left. Urban pondered how different the times were now. At one point in time, he would have declared absolutely no way on earth would he have done something like this with his brother. But right now? Maybe. It wasn't a bad idea, that's for sure. And it would certainly open up an awful lot of doors for him—if that's what he wanted.

Then, of course, Urban didn't know what he wanted. That was the problem. It all just seemed like too much right now. And maybe it was. Maybe he just needed to park all ideas, until he had a chance to think about it a bit more. So that's what he did tonight. He returned to his room and crashed. He didn't even wake up once.

AFTER ANOTHER FULL day of rehab, Urban had been thinking off and on about his brother's business proposal. But now Urban pondered it with his whole attention, as he rolled his way toward the dining room and dinner. That was the one thing that was always guaranteed to put a smile on his face, the food here. He meant to tell Dani about that at some point in time, but he still hadn't even made it that far yet.

It was kind of sad in a way because it just seemed as if there were opportunities here to do so much more in life, and he hadn't been necessarily looking at it with the right attitude. Not that it was a problem, just maybe not necessarily what he should be looking at. His brother David had a good eye for business. He'd already been involved in multiples of them, sold several, and made a couple small fortunes. His brother certainly didn't need Urban's money.

However, if David was interested in setting up some businesses with him, Urban would be a fool not to take advantage of that. Still, it was a commitment he wasn't sure he was ready to make.

"That's a long look on your face," Dennis noted.

Urban looked up at him, startled, and smiled. "Yeah, you're not kidding. My brother stopped by for a visit two days in a row," he shared, with a smile. "Nothing quite like family to shake things up."

At that, Shane stepped up behind him. "Your brother's a good guy. It was nice to see him."

"He is, indeed," Urban agreed, with a big smile. "He had a lot of good things to say about you too."

"We've known each other quite a while," he murmured. "And I didn't have a clue that he was your brother."

"Good thing you were treating me all right then, wasn't it?" Urban teased. "So I could tell him just that."

Shane laughed. "I would never expect anybody to lie when it came to the treatment they're getting here because I know that you're all getting exactly what you need."

Urban chuckled. "I wonder about that myself sometimes. Because are we? I would think so, but you never really know."

Shane gave him an odd look.

Urban shrugged. "Don't worry about me. I'm kind of in an odd mood."

"Family can do that," Shane noted.

"Yeah, they can at that." Shane waved goodbye, while Urban grabbed the plate from Dennis, not even sure what he'd asked for, and made his way slowly out onto the deck. As he pulled up to an empty table, he half hoped that he would get no company tonight. But, of course, that wasn't to be, and, maybe because he wanted no company, everybody came.

By the time his table was full up, he wondered at even thinking about getting peace and quiet tonight. Still, it was nice to have people to talk to sometimes. However, he had some things on his mind, and he had hoped to ease back a bit on socializing and have time to just let it all roll around in his brain, but it wasn't to be.

When he said good night to everybody and made his way back to his room, he was tired—not bothered, not upset, but slightly out of it. He wasn't even sure what to do about that. If he were at home, he would go to the gym, but being here felt odd. It didn't feel like something that he was supposed to do, and he suspected that his body already had more than enough of a workout today that he shouldn't really be putting it through any more of that kind of abuse.

As it was, what he really wanted was to see Bettina. And that felt odd too. He wasn't sure that he was supposed to be thinking along those lines, but, of course, it was hard for him not to. She was pretty special, and he knew it, even if he was slightly but deliberately distancing himself from her.

When a knock came on his door, he called out, "Come in." Still, he was kind of hoping that whoever it was would go away quickly—until he saw Bettina.

He beamed. "Now that's somebody I'm happy to see." She looked at him in surprise. He shrugged. "You know those times when you just want to be alone, and you hope that the rest of the world leaves you be, but then they don't, so you feel like you're an idiot for even hoping for it?"

She chuckled. "All of that today?" she asked, with a smile.

"Yeah, I know. It's pretty stupid, isn't it?"

"No, not at all," she murmured. "Nothing stupid here. Remember that."

"I dunno. It feels stupid today."

She walked closer to him. "Sounds like you're in an *off* mood."

"Yeah, and it's stupid. I don't know why. My brother came—two days in a row even—and would like me to go into business with him. And I know he's got a great reputation, so it'd be a really good opportunity, *blah-blah-blah-blah*." He waved his hands around.

"But you don't want to?"

"The problem is, I don't know what I want," he shared honestly. "And it just feels as going down this pathway is a commitment I'm not sure I want to make."

"Do you have to make that commitment now?" she asked.

"No, he would be fine to leave it for a while. I think he was …" He stopped. "I guess I'm afraid that he's making the offer because he doesn't think I'll have any other opportunities."

"Oh." Bettina frowned. "So it's not so much that you *don't* want to go into business with him, but that you're more worried about the *reasoning* behind his offer. Or are you afraid of being visible with your scars in the business world?"

"And that's foolish too, isn't it?" Urban stared at her. "Both reasons are."

"No, I don't think they're foolish at all," she disagreed. "I think it is important though for you to do what you need to do and not to do something because you think it's expected of you."

He smiled. "Yeah, I hear that. It's just weird."

"Life is weird for you right now," she murmured. "If you need something tonight to sleep, let me know."

"Sure. I guess you're at work right now, aren't you?" He added, "It's so weird to know that you're on night shift."

"It's weird, but it's also good," she replied. "It gives me freedom during the day to do things."

"And what do you do?" he asked curiously.

"I go to town. I rest. I read. I have a few hobbies I like to spend some time with. It's all about trying to bring balance to the world where I work. It can be pretty intense here at times, emotionally as well," she explained, "so it's just nice when I have a chance to get away a little bit."

"I can understand that. I'm just … We know so little about the staff, and you guys know so much about us."

"And it's not deliberate to keep you in the dark."

He nodded. "I get that. It's been a long time since I had time or energy or inclination to work on a *hobby,* so it's just a weird thought that you mention it right now."

"It is and it isn't," she murmured. "One of these days, you'll be on top of the world and wondering what you were worried about."

"Maybe, but that day isn't today."

"No, it isn't," she declared, with a defiant tone. "And, therefore, it's also not your worry of today."

He smiled. "Now if only that was as easy to brush off."

"It can be," she said cheerfully. "It's all up to how you want others in life to intrude. If you're not ready for the reality of it, then don't get sucked into it."

"And how do I *not,* when it's my brother?"

"Tell him that you're not ready to make that decision, that you'll look at it in a couple months."

"Oh, it would be nice to do that. Yet, at the same time, it kind of feels like a cop-out."

"No, it's defending your time right now. This is your healing time. You don't need to be worrying and thinking about all that."

"I don't know," he murmured. "It seems like I do."

"And, if you feel like you need to," she suggested, "then maybe you do. However, if you don't need to, then relax about it because not all of it has to be done right away." And, with that, she waved goodbye. "And now I'm back off to do rounds. I just popped in to see how your visit was."

"It was good. It was really nice to see him."

"And that's good to hear," she said. "Just make sure that you don't let him pressure you into doing something you don't want to do."

"No, he wouldn't do that. I might do that, but he wouldn't."

She chuckled. "Sometimes the biggest pressure is the pressure that we don't think is actually there—a subtle difference with friends and family."

"Maybe, I dunno."

She smiled. "I'll let you go. I've got to get back to work." And, with that, she was gone again.

Leaving him even more out of sorts than before.

Chapter 7

A S IT WAS, Bettina's evening was really busy, and then it was followed by two days off. By the time she came back to work, Urban had been on her mind steadily. She hadn't texted or checked in on him, trying to give him space and time to focus on what he felt he needed to do in his world. When she popped into his room, he looked up and frowned—almost as if not recognizing her—but then a smile broke across his face.

"I got really worried when I didn't see you," he said. "And then I realized that you work a job and that you get to leave this place, so that you have a life outside of here."

She nodded slowly. "I do. The same as you will soon."

He nodded and smiled. "I hope so."

"How have you been these last couple days? I'm sorry. I should have reminded you that I had days off."

He shook his head. "It's all right."

"It's all right perhaps." She sensed immediately that it was something she should have done. She'd wanted to, but she had been worried about crossing the lines. "I was just being super careful about following the rules and restrictions of the place," she explained, "and even then I'm not sure that I did that correctly."

He looked at her in surprise. "What do you mean?"

"At one point in time we had a rule about no relationships with patients," she shared, "and I know that that has eased up considerably. But I was thinking that, with all you had to think about, I didn't want to add to any of that, so, when I took my days off"—she raised both palms—"I didn't tell you that I was going. I just left. Yet I should have told you."

"I'm not your keeper," he noted, studying her carefully. "And I'm glad you had a chance to go away. I was half expecting, even though it was your day off, to see you around the place, maybe eating or swimming."

"And you're right. If you'd been down at the pool or the hot tub, that would have been a perfectly normal assumption," she replied. "As it was, I went into town and spent the day with a girlfriend."

"Oh, was that a fun time?"

"It was different," she noted, with a smile. "I haven't had a chance to spend much time with her lately. She's getting married and leaving town soon, so it was nice to see her."

"I'm sure it was," he agreed warmly. "And friendships like that are something that you should nourish to keep them flowing."

"Absolutely. And now that I'm back, my social life just feels very strange again."

"Of course." He chuckled. "Still, I'm glad you enjoyed the time you had."

"Thanks," she said, smiling. "And now, how about you?"

"I'm okay. It's been a hard-working couple days as always, and I had my first day off, which was also nice," he shared, giving her a big grin.

"It is nice to get a day off, no matter where in this world you're at," she declared. "And often these PT guys, even Shane, are good about it too."

"And often they're not," Urban declared with an eye roll. "Plus a day off away from Shane isn't necessarily good because I know that I will feel it when I go back tomorrow."

"Yeah, you probably will," she agreed, with a grimace. "That's just the way therapy works. The more you use your body, the better off you are. However, your body, once it's working hard, also needs to have a break."

"And I'm working it," he confirmed.

"Good," she murmured. "And now, I am once again back on duty, so I'll be running around and in and out of your life on a regular basis."

"Good," he said. As she headed to the door, he added, "I have to admit that I did miss you."

She glanced over at him and smiled. "I have to admit that I did miss you too." Then she gave a nervous chuckle, before walking out.

Bettina needed to leave his room because just hearing him say that brought a rush of emotions to her heart that she hadn't expected. He was a very special person, and yet, she reminded herself, he was a patient here. So she had to watch out for his emotions being triggered too because, well, sometimes the healing relationship was based on gratitude. So it could be a potential problem. When you got people who were injured and damaged, and they came to rely on everybody around them, sometimes it became a dependency scenario, and the patients sometimes saw something that was not really there.

For her sake, she hoped that wasn't the case with Urban because she liked everything about him. She hoped he truly felt the same way she did. He was very special, and she wanted to spend time with him, if she could. Yet she also knew instances where certain staff members were asked to stay away from certain patients because the relationship had taken a turn that wasn't healthy for the patient. And Bettina didn't want that in Urban's case. Couldn't hurt to just be friends or at least to see how far down that pathway he went.

With that thought in mind, she headed for Shane's rehab area and found him writing up notes.

He looked up and smiled at her. "Hey, how were your days off?"

"They were good. How is Urban doing?"

"He's doing fine." Shan studied her and grinned. "I do hear a special note in that tone of yours."

"He's a special guy," she said. "We hit it off right on his first day."

"Good." Shane nodded. "Something like that's always good for them, to know they aren't alone."

"Yeah, I just worry that I'm interfering in his recovery."

He looked up at her in surprise and shook his head. "I haven't seen any sign of it. … Believe me. If I do, you'll be the first to know."

She winced at that. "And I would just as soon not have anything like that happen."

He nodded. "I get that—and appreciate it. However, I think, at this point in time, you're worrying too much."

"I hope so." Bettina smiled. "I would hate to think that it was a problem."

"I don't think so," he repeated. "All is well at the moment."

"Glad to hear it. I'll let you get back to your records." And, with that, she left him alone.

Smiling was about all she could do, plus hope that Shane was right. She kept up the friendliness with Urban, and also kept an eye on him a little bit closer than she normally would for most of her patients, so stopping in to see if he wanted anything from the kitchen from time to time, just for an excuse to pop by and visit.

When she caught him looking at a bunch of paperwork, she frowned. "Wow, that looks serious."

"It's all the forms from my brother."

"Forms?" she asked.

"Yeah, remember? About the business stuff."

"Ah, that sounds interesting."

He nodded. "He seems to be pretty serious about me going into business with him."

"Are you still hesitating?"

"No, I'm not hesitating about going into business with him. I think I'm just hesitating about that whole *going into business* thing."

"And that's understandable," she murmured. "Again, don't pressure yourself into deciding too much at once." And, with that, she was gone again. She wasn't sure if she was escaping or just trying to not influence his decision.

When she popped back in again, he looked up and smiled. "I hardly even get a chance to talk to you."

"Honestly, it's just been crazy this shift," she replied, "but I've also been giving you some space, so you can work through the business stuff."

"Oh, my goodness." He frowned at her. "You don't have to do that."

"I just want to make sure that I won't influence you one way or another," she stated.

He shook his head. "Nope, I wouldn't make decisions like that so quickly anyway. However, there is a reason why the thought does appeal. I tried a fair bit of business ventures and completed several business courses before I went into the navy," he shared. "I was fairly entrepreneurial even back then, and I considered it before enlisting, but I had a different cause in my heart. And now that I've had another chance to consider what I want to do," he added, "going back to a business does kind of appeal. I'm just not sure yet. I guess the question is, what kind of business do I want to get into, and will I want to stay in that for years to come?"

"And, of course, that's not something to rush," she murmured.

"Nope, it definitely isn't. And yet it's something that people everywhere do think about, wondering if they are in the right career, wondering what the right field might be for them." He gave her a smile. "But you definitely don't have to worry about influencing me."

"Good. In that case, I was about to run to the dining room and see if I could steal an ice cream."

He repeated, "Ice cream?"

She looked at him and nodded. "Surely you've had one of Dennis's ice creams."

"*Nooo.*" His eyes widened in mock outrage. "You're telling me there's ice cream to be had here, and I didn't know about it?"

"Do you like ice cream?"

"Yeah, which is probably why everybody kept the news from me," he teased, a smile on his face.

"Maybe." She smirked. "So any particular flavor?"

"No, I don't even know what might be available, but I'll take one if you got one coming."

"I'll see." She left his room and headed to the dining area, a smile on her face.

Dennis took one look and shook his head. "*Uh-oh,* are you raiding my ice cream fridge again?"

"Absolutely, one for me and one for Urban, if possible."

"Wow, you two are really sweet on each other, aren't you?" he asked, with a big grin.

She gave him an eye roll. "You're not the first to mention that."

"Hey, I've seen so many relationships happen here," he noted, "that I'd be surprised if it *didn't* happen." She tilted her head at him. He nodded. "Not everybody sees how it all happens, but, considering where I'm situated, I get the bird's-eye view of most of them." He chuckled.

"That's not a bad thing either."

"No, not at all," he agreed. "Matter of fact, I think it's quite a good thing. I've been a big proponent of love surmounting all battles, so it always makes my heart smile to see relationships happen. And, if you and Urban are hitting it off, that's even better."

"We're hitting it off," she shared. "I'm just not sure where it's going."

"And don't put that restraint on it right now. Let it run, let it ride, go with the waves, and just see what comes," Dennis murmured. "You might be surprised. It could be something so wonderful that you realize how much you've missed all your life."

"That would be nice," she agreed. "For the longest time I figured I was well past it." He frowned at her. She shrugged and added, "When you don't have a relationship for a long time, you wonder if maybe something's wrong with you. And, if so, what are you supposed to do about it?" She brought up her hands, showing her palms. "It's not an easy thing to solve."

"No, it sure isn't," he noted, with a wide grin. "However, I'm a big fan of just letting things happen, being open to seeing what comes, and, when it does, recognizing it when it's there."

"Even when recognizing it, how do you know if it's real?" she asked. "I don't have anything to go on for experience."

"Ah." Dennis nodded. "And what's his experience like?"

"I have no idea," she admitted, "but, given that he's in this situation here—where healing him creates a special bond but not necessarily a true romantic one—I'm not sure that he's a good judge either."

"There's always that concern about making sure that they're not seeing you as something you aren't and not putting you into a gratitude type of relationship," Dennis noted. "I do think most people understand where they're coming from better than that. … I think we sometimes don't give them the benefit of the doubt."

"Maybe," she hedged. "It still won't get you out of giving us ice cream."

He rolled his eyes her way. "You know that, if you guys keep stealing my ice cream, we'll run out."

"Then you'll just order more," she stated cheerfully.

He gave a shout of laughter at that. "Maybe, just maybe. Anyway, one scoop or two?"

"Two," she decided instantly.

"At least you're eating," he murmured. And, with that, he disappeared.

She walked over, studied the coffee, and wondered if she could carry back coffee and treats. No, better to have the treats and then coffee afterward. And, when she turned around, there was Dennis, standing with a double set of large cones. "Is that two scoops?" she asked, staring at it in amazement.

"Yep. At least it's two scoops for today," he clarified, chuckling.

She shook her head. "Wow. I'll probably be back for coffee in a little bit." And, with that, walking carefully down the hallway and hoping not too many people saw her, she made it back to Urban's room. She struggled to knock on the door, when somebody popped up beside her and knocked for her.

"Don't know where you got that ice cream," Shane noted, "but wow."

"I know," she murmured. "And I won't tell you because I'll just get in trouble."

"You'll get in trouble anyway," he stated, "because I'm about to go tell Dennis that you've got them."

She burst out laughing. "And who do you think gave them to me?"

"What?" he asked in mock horror. "In that case, I'll go get one myself." When Urban said a belated "Come in," Shane opened the door for her. And then off he went.

Bettina stepped into the room and smiled at Urban.

"Was that Shane I just heard?"

"Yes, he saw me with these," she said, with a big smile.

He took one look and shook his head. "Wow."

"Right?" she murmured. "Isn't that just unbelievable?"

"Those are unbelievably huge," he agreed, "and they look delicious."

"That's Dennis for you," she said, with a smile. "And no reason why they can't be huge here," she added, "so it's all good."

"True. This place is pretty special regardless."

"It is, indeed. Now, here is your cone. Do you want it here or do you want to go for a ride?"

He frowned at her. "Do you have time?"

"I do. I have about fifteen minutes."

He shook his head. "No, in that case, I don't want to share you with anybody. I would just as soon spend that time here with you."

She looked at him in surprise, but it was hard not to be pleased at his words. "And that is a very sweet thing to say," she murmured.

He shrugged. "I don't know about sweet, but it's the truth."

And she believed him. And it made her heart smile with joy.

URBAN WAS REALLY enjoying his time with Bettina. It felt right. Natural. They'd fallen into a regular pattern, where she would stop in as soon as she came on shift, see if he wanted anything, spend a few minutes with him if she happened to be early enough, and then she'd pop in several times throughout the evening. When it was her time off, she would nap, swim, eat, and then usually try to fit in lunch with him. And he was really looking forward to sharing a meal with her in the middle of the day.

Even Shane noticed. "Look. If you put in the effort," Shane suggested, "I can let you go a few minutes early."

Urban stared at him. "Sorry?"

"Come on. I can definitely tell that you're waiting for an opportunity to go to lunch with her."

"That's true," Urban admitted, with a sheepish grin. "It is nice to know that somebody out there cares."

"Hey," Shane pointed out, "I care." Then he gave Urban

a knowing grin. "We all do here. That's why we show up every day."

"Okay, okay, but there is a difference with Bettina."

"Absolutely there is," Shane agreed gently. "Just make sure that it's emotional and heartfelt love and not just gratitude."

"I heard that mentioned before. Blows me away that anybody can get those two mixed up. My fear would be more that it's not a relationship she wants to go further with," he noted, with difficulty.

"And why would you think that?" Shane asked.

"Just because she has so many more opportunities than I do. And I feel as if I have to make changes, and she probably isn't thinking of the same type of changes."

"Meaning?"

"I don't know. I'm just … I'm in a state of flux, and I don't know where I'll end up with it down the road," he shared, with a gentle shrug. "And I don't want to broach the topic about a future, just in case her answer is not what I want to hear, and it'll set me back. The last thing I want is for any relationship to blow up in my face and to have that impact my healing."

"Not something I want either," Shane agreed. "That would be seriously bad."

"I know, right? So Bettina and I are just kind of playing it by ear and seeing how all this goes."

"And I agree with that too," Shane said. "It's important to be happy in the process."

"And I am," Urban declared. "It's really nice to have even just a friend, a special friend, in a place like this. It's not something I ever expected."

"Understood." Shane gave him a bright smile. "Let me

know how you guys get along."

"BETTINA AND I are doing fine," Urban told Shane a few days later. "However, sometimes I think *fine* means it's not good."

"Wow," Shane replied. "Seriously?"

"I don't know. I just, … when I was younger, it was all about dynamic relationships and excitement and passion," he shared. "And, honest to God, right now, being around her is like seeing another part of me," he shared, "and I want that to be real and honest. However, at the same time, I'm not exactly sure what all that means. It's just so very different."

"*Different* doesn't have to be bad."

"No, it's not bad," Urban corrected, "because a serenity, a peace is in my heart that I never had before. Also a know-ingness in my heart that I've never experienced before. And again I think it all goes back to comparing the me in the present time to that whole younger self. … Maybe there's just maturity here."

"I can agree with that," Shane replied. "You're also changing, and what you wanted back then versus what you want now is very different."

"I hope so." Urban wore a great big smile. "She's a special person, and I really don't want to lose that relationship."

"No reason why you should," Shane noted.

"That's what I was hoping, but it feels very strange to be talking about something like this, especially when I've been through so much. Plus, this dating part of my life wasn't even something in my thought processes."

"And maybe these special relationships are important

enough that they should be here now," he murmured.

"And it is special. No doubt about it, it is. I just …" And then he broke off. "I guess I just hadn't expected to want something so very different in this stage in my life."

Shane laughed. "Maybe you are more surprised that what you thought you wanted is not what Bettina is at all. At this stage of your life," Shane added, "maybe you were expecting the same old, same old, yet you got something very different. Regardless, you want somebody to be there long-term. You want somebody who'll know what it's like to see you at your worst but to understand it anyway. You want somebody who'll be there on the rocking chair beside you, helping you get through the good times and the bad times."

"But not just her being there for me. I want her to know that I will be there for her too," Urban murmured. "It seems so easy to dismiss that, but, after what I've been through, it's a seriously important element that I would never even have thought to want in another relationship."

"And I think that's important to recognize too. When you think about it, do you want to date again? After Bettina, I mean."

"Heavens no. At the same time, my relationship with Bettina is definitely something that I want for right now and that I want to see go long-term."

Shane nodded. "Got it. For the record, she isn't some-body who's had other relationships here, I don't think. I'm pretty sure she's very much of the opinion that one time around is perfect."

Urban chuckled. "Me too. … It's just a matter of mak-ing sure you get it right during that *one time around*." And still smiling, they finished the workout, and Urban got ready for lunch.

As he made his way slowly in the wheelchair down to the dining area he was stopped by a visit from a 3 legged cat who chose him for a cuddle. The cat jumped into his lap as if he was sure of his welcome. Scratching the furry belly after it was presented as if the cat absolutely knew he was there for just that reason made his day. Still smiling he carried on the cafeteria. At the double doors the cat hopped off and walked to someone else for his daily dose of love.

Bettina looked up from her table at him and waved him over.

"I just had a visit from a three legged cat." He grinned at her. "He just jumped up, got his cuddle and left."

"Yep he's good at that. I think there are a couple around here with three legs now. You should be happy – you were chosen today." She smiled brightly at him on to have it dim a moment later. "Hey, you look pretty pensive," she noted.

"Just realizing I've been here over a month already," he said. "One month ago I didn't even know who you were."

She smiled. "So maybe today is a good day."

"It's a very good day," he agreed. "I just wonder what the next two to three months will bring."

"As much as you want them to," she murmured. "Or at least as much as you might handle day to day."

He smiled. "That's what I'm hoping for. It's pretty hard to remember feeling so alone just a short thirty days ago."

She laced her fingers with his and whispered, "But you're not alone now, so just relax."

"I get that," he murmured. "Just, every once in a while, it strikes me how different my life was, how lonely it was."

"And the good news is," she added, "that time has passed."

"Yep, absolutely," he declared, with a bright smile. "And

what were you doing a month ago?"

"I was contemplating going to another town for some extra training," she replied, with a shrug. "Just something that came up in a conversation with Dani."

"And are you still thinking about it?"

She nodded. "I am. I'll be gone for about a week."

"Go," he urged. "I'll miss you terribly, but I think it's important that you continue to gain education and training."

"And I plan on it," Bettina added. "I just hadn't finalized it with Dani yet."

"Oh, I think it'd be lovely if you could," Urban suggested. "And nice that you're still talking about professional development. So many people, once they get into their field, don't want to improve anymore."

"I don't think that's something you will find here," she noted. "So many of us are very aware of our shortcomings in dealing with the level of trauma we see here, not to mention the emotional adjustments required of all the patients, which we tend to forget are some adjustments required of us too. There's always something we can improve on."

Chapter 8

BETTINA DID SIGN up for the conference. Before she attended it though, she walked into Urban's room to update him. "Hey. Remember. I'm leaving soon."

He looked up, a little distracted from his paperwork. "Right, the conference." He smiled and nodded. "Go and enjoy yourself."

"And you'll be just fine while I'm gone."

"It won't be the same though," he shared.

She added, "At least it's only five days."

He agreed. "It is only five days. But, at the moment, five days seems like a long time."

Unfortunately it seemed like forever, Bettina thought, from his point of view. But she was bound and determined to keep up the bright smile and the happy tone of voice for him. "Remember. It won't be long," she said, "and you can always text me."

"Will do," he replied. "But let's forget about it for now and head off for dinner. I'm starving."

"Good enough." She was a little worried that he was pushing off her five-day absence, but maybe it was just an easier way to deal with it. Maybe it was really no big deal for him. That bothered her more than anything. She would prefer to think, if she were gone for five days, that he would care. And, of course, no way he wouldn't care, but his reaction just then felt odd.

She groaned as they walked up to the buffet line.

Dennis took one look and asked, "What's that for?"

"It'll be my last meal here for the next few days," she explained, with a slight grimace. "I'm heading off to that conference."

"Right." Dennis nodded. "I remember that. So what'll it be?" he asked. "After this, it'll only be conference food for you."

She shuddered. "Most of the time it's not so bad, but lately? Man, those conference meals have been pretty rough."

"That's because they're not serving my food," Dennis teased.

"I know, and that's a little more distressing than I care to admit right now." Then she saw they were having steak and smiled. "Oh, I could get behind a steak."

"And I've got them out on the barbecue on the deck. How do you want yours?"

"Medium rare," she replied, with a big smile.

"Good enough." Dennis looked over at Urban. "What about you?"

"Medium rare for me too. Have you got a grill on?" Urban asked.

"I do, indeed," Dennis stated, "and Ilse is out there right now."

"Sounds good," Urban murmured. They headed outside to the smell of grilling steak.

"Wow," Bettina murmured, as Urban rolled over to Ilse.

He asked, "Don't suppose you have any peppers you could throw on there, do you?"

She nodded at him. "Absolutely. Anything else you want?"

"Zucchini, maybe a tomato?"

Ilse chuckled. "Grilled vegetables coming up." She looked over at Bettina. "Do you want a few?"

"I've never had any grilled veggies, so yes."

"Perfect." And Ilse headed back inside and returned within seconds with a large bowl of vegetables. While she stood here watching the steaks, she quickly trimmed them up and quartered the peppers and tossed them on, along with the zucchini cut in long slices. Then she brushed them with oil and some seasoning. By the time she had those done, several other people had gathered around, asking about them. "If I'd known you guys wanted grilled veggies, I could have set this up from the beginning."

"Hey, it's all right," Urban noted. "We appreciate the effort."

"Good, but, hey, I'm working on it right now. So give me a few minutes, and I'll get a bunch of these out." And that's what she did, while they all stood around and waited. "Go grab baked potatoes and all the fixings inside, plus your salads," she suggested, "and, by the time you're done, I should have this pretty-well beat."

Almost as if a mad charge had been ordered, everybody headed inside, looking for the sides to their meal. And by the time they all came back outside, Ilse was busy pulling steaks off and dishing them up. When she got to Urban, she smiled and said, "You are the one who started all this." And she filled his plate with peppers and zucchini and a grilled tomato.

URBAN LOOKED AT it and sighed happily. "I don't think

there's anything quite like grilled veggies."

"Maybe not." Ilse chuckled. "We'll do this again," she promised.

At that, he smiled. "Now that would be nice." Obviously it wasn't a bad idea. "Also, I haven't seen anything like potato salad come up on the menus so far."

She nodded. "If you want potato salad, I can do you up potato salad. How do you feel about *baked* potato salad?"

He looked at her in surprise, looked down at the baked potato on his plate, and asked, "Is that a thing?"

"It's absolutely a thing."

"Hey, it's all good."

She nodded. "We're always looking for ideas. A suggestion box is on the side wall over there." She pointed it out. "Anytime you get a craving for some particular item, let me know. And I'll try to work it into the menu."

With a wave, Urban headed over to the table where Bettina sat, working on decking out her baked potato. He pulled up beside her. "They're really, really amiable here."

"It's one big family," she agreed, with a nod. "And it's one of the reasons why I'm working toward professional development. I always want to be relevant, so I can always have a job here."

He frowned at her and nodded. "I hadn't considered that, but, of course, new techniques mean new training, and they must always have the best of the best, don't they?"

"They absolutely do," she stated, followed by a sigh, "and that's not the easiest thing to maintain."

"No, of course not." He reached across, grabbed her hand, and said, "I'll miss you."

"And I will miss you too," she replied. And then she cut into her steak, put a piece in her mouth, and closed her eyes.

"Oh my God." He did the same but to a bell pepper. She stared at his pepper.

He pointed to hers and said, "Try it."

She took a bite, and her eyes widened. "They're so sweet."

"Yes, that's one of the things about barbecuing that I love," he explained. "It brings out a completely different aspect of the vegetable."

"It's wonderful," she murmured. "Absolutely wonderful."

He smiled, noting how much easier his smiles were coming. Hathaway House was good for him. He could even acknowledge how much he was coming out of his shell, not so self-conscious about his facial scarring; more to the point, he wasn't sure he even had a protective shell anymore. Seemed he was finally seeing himself as *normal*. "Glad to hear that you liked the grilled veggies. And now you know that it's something worth trying again."

"I can see a whole variety of vegetables worth trying this way," she murmured. "This is amazing."

"Good." He smiled again and tucked into his meal.

At the same time there was almost a sad atmosphere to the evening, as Bettina was leaving early in the morning. By the time their dinner was done, she accompanied him back to his room, seeing the fatigue in his eyes that he wouldn't admit to. She shared, "I'm leaving now."

"You're not on night shift tonight?"

She shook her head. "No, because I'm traveling all day tomorrow, so I've got tonight off."

He nodded. "Okay."

She smiled but felt awkward. She was too physically distant for him to give a hug or a kiss, but, at the same time, she didn't want to be the first one to make a move. As she walked to the door, she said, "Now make sure you look after yourself."

"Hey, I'm not the one traveling," he noted. "I'll be here, still doing the same old thing."

"Spend time with others." She stopped, looked at him, and then walked back over, reached down, and gave him a big hug. "Just look after yourself, you big galoot." And, with that, she disappeared.

THE NEXT MORNING and even the rest of the day, all day, Urban kept waiting for her to pop in. Yet he knew that she wasn't even close by. He tried hard not to get down about it, but it wasn't easy. At times he definitely just wanted to sit in his room and be morose. Even Shane worked him harder, almost as if he knew how Urban felt.

By the third day without Bettina, Urban groaned and complained to Shane, "Are you deliberately trying to kill me?"

"No, I'm just confirming that you are not depressed, isolated, or starting to slump because she's not here."

"You would never let me do that," Urban noted, with an eye roll. "And I would still have to answer to her when she got back."

At that, Shane laughed. "I hadn't thought of that. She won't let you off the hook either, will she?"

"Nope, not at all. And I do miss her," Urban admitted.

"And that's good. You're supposed to miss her." Shane chuckled. "It means you care."

"Yeah, and you don't really realize it, not until somebody goes away like this."

"Very true, and, at the same time, absence is supposed to make the heart grow fonder."

"*Uh-oh*," Urban moaned, "then I'm in trouble."

At that, Shane laughed. "You'll be fine. It's only a week."

"Five days," Urban corrected.

Shane turned to him, his grin twitching at the corners of his mouth. "In five days we could have you walking. How do you feel about that?"

Urban frowned at him. "I don't think so."

"I didn't say walking *well* but walking."

Urban still frowned but added, "If I could even walk into the dining room with her one day, that would be lovely."

"There's no *one day* about it," Shane clarified. "We've had to realign a lot of body parts, but it's almost time for you to get back up on your feet and start to do things different-ly."

"Good," Urban replied. "I am kind of walking ever-so-slightly but not much."

"Explain."

"Just at night," Urban replied. "I went to the bathroom last night. I just got up and grabbed one crutch and made my way there," he explained.

"Perfect," Shane declared. "I really like to hear that. How did it feel?"

"It felt good. It felt kind of scary, but it also felt very enlivening."

"And that's perfect," Shane added. "It's important for you to remember that the wheelchair is temporary. It becomes an extension of yourself, but it also becomes a crutch that becomes too easy."

"Nothing is easy about a wheelchair," he argued, shaking his head.

"No, but it's a lot easier than the scariness about being back on your feet and falling again."

Urban winced at that. "I hear you. At the same time it's also, as you mentioned, it's a little unnerving to realize that I'm supposed to trust this body while vertical again."

"And that's why we take it slow, and, after that, it will be fine again. And you'll gain confidence in what your ability is."

"I'm glad to hear that," he murmured, "because it doesn't really feel as if I'm doing so well right now."

"You're doing fine. I don't know why you feel like you aren't, but you're doing just fine."

"Good. Yet, at the same time, I've been fine even though I haven't been walking."

"And we will get you back on your feet and show you that you've already made some progress, so it won't be as bad as you're expecting."

"I hope not, because I really want that. I just know that the confidence isn't right there for me."

"And that's fine," Shane murmured. "Just take it easy, and you'll do fine."

Chapter 9

T HE CONFERENCE WAS fascinating and entertaining and definitely kept her going for the first couple days, which was good because she kept thinking about what Urban was doing and how everybody back home was. They really were *home* to her; they really were her family. And yet how fascinating that she could do two things at once—keeping him in her mind, even as she kept working away at improving her job skills.

It was absolutely important to her that she stay at Hathaway House, and that meant keeping her skills always current and always up-to-date, with the latest and the best because the patients deserved that. She firmly believed that, and she knew that everybody else there did too. And, when one fostered that responsibility in that atmosphere in the staff, as Dani had, it made everybody want to do so much more. Bettina wanted to work with more people like Urban. She could do so much more and would enjoy watching as they improved. But she worried about what Urban would do, when he was gone. She knew it was months away yet, but how did one even get past that?

By the time she was ready to head home, she was so ready in so many other ways. She'd texted him several times, but it wasn't the same.

She had deliberately avoided long phone calls because

she didn't want him worrying about her and even taking her attention away from what she had to do. Still, she couldn't wait to get home. The conference was great and all, but enough was enough. She loved to travel, but she loved to come home after traveling even more. There was just something great about getting away and having a break, but something was even so much better about having a chance to get home and to see everybody again, particularly Urban.

He was special, and that was driving her crazy because she just wanted to spend every moment with him. She couldn't figure out whether that was a good thing or a bad thing. She just knew that she was well past the point of even making a decision about it. He was there for her in all ways, and she just needed to be there for him.

By the time she got off the plane and grabbed her car from the long-term parking and started the drive to the center, she felt a sense of anticipation like she hadn't expected. She and Urban had only met, not even two months ago. It was too early for them to be making long-term decisions, yet it was incredible to know that he was there and that she would be spending as much time with him over the next while as she could. Hopefully they would find out if they were right for each other. And how did one do that except spend time together?

She realized just what a gift Hathaway House was all over again because not only was he there, he was learning and improving, and becoming a completely different person, but she was there on the spot, watching that growth and that improvement. Not every relationship got that opportunity. Most relationships never got that opportunity. It was just too far-fetched for them to see each other in all these aspects, unless when recovering from an injury like this. She understood fully how nurses fell in love with their patients. Bettina just had never had anyone make her feel the way Urban did.

To think that she was in love after so many years of thinking that it would never happen to her sent her into absolute delight and absolute fear at the same time. What if she was wrong? What if she was making a mistake and this wasn't really what was happening? Maybe he didn't really feel that way.

It would be devastating for her, if that's not how he felt. She couldn't even contemplate thinking that way, and yet how was she *not* supposed to worry? Absolutely no way to know about those things. It would take time for them to work through their issues, whatever those issues were. And to figure out just how to deal with something like this. Just because she wanted to jump into it didn't mean that was the way to do it.

However, neither did she want Urban to feel like absolutely nothing was there for him. She wanted him to know that she was there for him in all ways. Still, it was too early. She didn't want to hold back his healing, and she didn't want him to heal just for her. She needed him to believe fully in them. And to believe in so many other things that they could do.

How did one do that? She didn't know, but she was willing to find out. Urban had to feel the same way she did; anything less would just kill her. Especially when she'd waited this long.

If only she would get to Hathaway House while he was still awake. As she checked her watch, she realized that it wouldn't be fair to disturb him tonight. It was already ten o'clock. When she finally pulled in front of her apartment, she parked and walked inside. As soon as she opened the door, she smiled. Now this was home. And nothing filled her heart with more warmth than to know that she was here. She pulled out her phone and sent him a text message. **I made it.**

She got a happy emoji back, and then he texted **I'm still up, if you want to come for a visit.**

She frowned at that.

And then he added, **Herb tea on the dining room deck?**

She laughed and sent him an immediate response. **Yes, be there in five.** And she quickly brought in her stuff from the car and headed to the dining room. He wasn't there when she arrived, so she made her tea and walked out onto the deck, where she sat down, taking deep, slow breaths to acknowledge that she was home again.

When she heard something but wasn't quite sure what, she turned to see him slowly making his way toward her on crutches. She bolted to her feet, her hands on her cheeks, as she stared at him in joy. "Oh my, to think what you accomplished when I wasn't even here."

He chuckled. "Hey, I'm not walking without crutches yet, but that's definitely part of the goal."

"I would think so," she murmured, tears in her eyes. "This is amazing."

He smiled. "Thanks, I was hoping I could make it for when you got back."

"If that's your goal," she said, her voice thickening, "you succeeded." She walked over, gave him a hug. "Now please, sit down before you fall down."

He burst out laughing. "See? You're always honest with me."

"Of course I am. How can I not be? You've done so much that it's just amazing."

He smiled at her. "I have to admit that I'm pretty stoked about it myself."

"And you should be," she declared. "It's absolutely amazing what you have managed to do."

He smiled. "Thank you." He beamed. "I'm so glad you're home."

"Me too," she murmured. "Even more so now that I see how well you've done. I'm a little jealous that I didn't see this happening in stages."

"Not to worry," he said. "Some serious time frames are coming for me to show you some real progress. We're close, just not there yet."

"And that matters," she murmured. "It so matters."

"Absolutely." He looked at the hot water. "I need to make a cup of tea."

"Don't bother. I already made you one." And she held out a second cup.

He smiled at her. "See? We're so in sync already."

"Always," she whispered in a teary voice. "Always."

SOMETIMES ALL THE best-laid plans still went wrong. And that's how Urban felt when he woke up in the middle of the next night, his body screaming in agony. He lay stiff, scared to even breathe in case something went wrong. And yet he could only do so much before he finally reached for the button, crying out in agony. And, of course, guess who came to his rescue?

Bettina opened the door, gasped, and came running.

He whispered in agony, "My back—it seized."

She pulled away the blanket to take a look at his back

and then said, "Hang on. I'll be right back."

He lay there, sweat dripping off his forehead, scared to even breathe too hard in case it expanded his chest and caused him excruciating pain. When more footsteps ran toward him, Urban recognized Shane's voice.

Shane groaned as he entered. "Looks like you did too much, *huh?*"

"Yeah." Urban gasped.

She held out two pills. "Can you pop these in?" He opened his mouth without question, and she held a straw in a cup, so he could swallow them with some water.

As soon as that was down, he laid still, his body completely rigid. Within minutes he heard an oddly recognizable sound, as Shane put some oil on his hands and immediately started working Urban's completely locked-up body. Just his hands on his body was sheer agony. And Urban could only do so much to hold back the pain. He was painfully stiff, and yet he didn't want her to see him this way. Finally he heard muted voices, followed by somebody leaving, her footsteps walking away.

And then Shane spoke. "Now you can relax. She's gone."

Urban shuddered with the pain. "How did you know?"

"Because I'm male too," he replied, "and it's hard to show emotion."

"I'm bawling like a baby in the pillow."

"Good, if that's what you need to do, then that's what you need to do," Shane declared. "I'll have this worked out of you pretty quickly, but it will take a few minutes."

It was longer than a few minutes, but then they both knew it would be. And still, it just didn't seem to make any difference, not until finally Urban could stretch out his legs. Shane moved them into different angles, just gently easing up the tightness.

When Urban could breathe, and it didn't kill him, he took another cautious breath, and that seemed to be fine too. And he slowly started to relax.

"Better?" Shane asked.

"Yeah," Urban breathed, "much."

"Good, and now the question is, what did you do?"

"What did I do?" he repeated. "I used crutches and walked down to see her tonight. She'd just gotten in and told me that she was here, and I wanted to meet for a cup of tea on the deck."

"*Ouch*. We were hoping you could walk by the time she got home, but we hadn't really cleared you on it," Shane replied calmly.

"No, and here I thought that I could be the big man that I am and could get there on my own anyway. Serves me right for trying to show off." He moaned slightly. "As if I needed any more awareness about how far I still had to go."

"And that doesn't matter. It'll happen. Another time," Shane stated. "You attempted to do something, and it didn't work out. Don't keep racking yourself over it."

"Easy for you to say." Urban groaned. "It's not working out so well for me."

Shane chuckled. "No, but I appreciate the fact that it was worth the effort to try to get down there and then to get back."

"It wasn't bad, at the time," he muttered. "Yet it hasn't been very easy since I woke up."

"Now let's see if you can roll onto your back."

It was a slow process, mostly because Urban was afraid that every movement would jerk the pain back through his body again. However, as he slowly rotated and collapsed onto his back, he did so with relief. "I hope that never happens again."

"It could," Shane admitted calmly. "You know yourself that, when you go too far with something, it tends to come back and bite you in the butt."

"Wouldn't be so bad if it was just the butt," he quipped, "but it felt as if this thing wanted chunks of everything I have."

Shane gave him a gentle smile in return. "Now, do you think you can sleep?"

"I don't know," he muttered. "I'm still too scared to move."

"I hear you. I'm just hoping that it's not anything too bad. We'll find out tomorrow. We'll just do a much easier schedule and mostly a lot of stretching," Shane added. "You'll be sore when you wake up, so get out of bed gently."

"Yeah, do you think I'll make it through the night with the painkillers and the anti-inflammatory?"

"Yes, and the muscle relaxants she's gone to get you will help too."

"If you say so," he muttered. Then came a gentle tap on the door, and, sure enough, it was Bettina again.

She came in, and, when she saw him, a bright smile crossed her face. "Oh, good," she said, with relief. "I'm so sorry, but at least you're feeling better."

"Hey, it happens," he murmured. He accepted the medication and swallowed it back.

"Do you think you can sleep?" she asked. "You want a cup of tea or something?"

He shook his head. "I think I'll probably be fine." And she quickly disappeared for her rounds.

Urban looked over at Shane. "Thanks."

"Yep," he murmured. "You're lucky that I was checking on another patient, somebody who's new, who's having a lot of trouble on his arrival. So I was here to help you out too."

"And what would happen if you weren't?"

"Somebody else would come in, but it would have taken longer," Shane noted. "You know we would like to think that we get the chance to sleep ourselves, but it doesn't always happen."

"Fat chance," he muttered. "I can't imagine that you get very much sleep sometimes."

"We try hard." Shane chuckled. "Remember. Don't interrupt your sleep to show up for breakfast. No rushing anywhere, and we'll work on stretching tomorrow." And, with that, Shane was gone.

Urban sank back on the bed, the drying tears still in the corners of his eyes and on his cheeks. That had been brutal. And, if he ever needed a reminder that he was a long way away from being an independent, mobile, and healed male, that was it. But eventually, by slowly relaxing a little farther with each breath, he fell back asleep again.

Chapter 10

THE NEXT DAY, just before her shift started, Bettina walked into Urban's room, but it was empty. Frowning, and yet not really expecting him necessarily to always be in his room, she looked around Hathaway House for him, but she saw no sign of him. She returned to his room, dropped him a little note on his pillow, and headed to her shift. She would stop at the dinner break to see if he was around. Yet at dinnertime there was no sign of him either. As she walked in the dining area to grab herself some food, she looked over at Dennis and asked, "Have you seen Urban?"

He nodded. "He's taking it very easy today, spent a lot of the time in the hot tub."

She rolled her eyes. "Of course. That's the one place I didn't even think to check."

"Ha. That's definitely a place you should be looking for that guy. He does love his water."

"He does, indeed." She grabbed her dinner and walked out onto the deck, placed it on a table, and then looked down at the pool area. Sure enough, Urban was stretched out in the hot tub, seemingly asleep. She picked up her dinner and walked downstairs, where she pulled a small table over beside him. "May I join you?" she whispered.

His eyelids flew open, and he looked at her and smiled. "Always," he said. "I would love to be eating too, but anything I do seems to just bring on more pain."

"And I presume Shane knows about it?"

"Oh, yeah, we've been working on it all day," he admitted. "Apparently my stunt last night—to show you how well I was doing—backfired."

"But you certainly don't need to be showing off for me," she said calmly. "I know exactly where you're at for progress, and I am grateful that you can see the progress yourself and that you would want to show off, but it's not necessary."

"Maybe not necessary," he conceded, "but it sure would have been nice. Or it would have been nice if there weren't repercussions."

She nodded and smiled. "You'll get there when your body is ready," she stated. "No rush."

"No, just me, anxious to get on with life."

"And I'm quite happy to have you here for as long as you need to be here," she noted gently.

He chuckled. "In a way, it just makes life easier for us."

"Sometimes it's certainly convenient." And she smiled, as she kept that in mind while going through her shift, even during her days, because it was convenient to stop in and to see him whenever. No, he wasn't always in his room, and that was a little disturbing because she worried immediately that something had gone wrong. She had other patients who did have things going wrong that she was certainly aware could happen; she just didn't want it to happen to anybody and definitely didn't want to see Urban suffer any more than he had up until now.

She loved the fact that he had wanted to have tea out on the deck with her, but, when he mentioned it again on another night, she shook her head firmly. "No, you need to sleep."

"I have been sleeping," he murmured. "I'm much better."

She chuckled. "That would be nice, but I'm not sure I believe you."

He gasped in wide-eyed mock horror.

She smiled and shook her head. "No, not this time. We need you better than ever. No setbacks."

He raised both hands in surrender. "Fine, but I really didn't think the aftermath was that bad."

"Now you're lying," she said immediately.

He chuckled. "I am. I would dearly love to never have that scenario happen again."

"Good, then we need to work on it and to get you on your feet and back up, so that you can try walking again," she stated, "but only when your body's ready."

He nodded. "Whenever that will be, it seems like a long shot these days."

"That's only because it's easy to get in a rush."

"That is true," he admitted. "I wasn't really thinking of how long away everything can be."

"It can be seemingly *forever* in some cases," she teased, still smiling. "However, we know that you're heading in the right direction, and that's what counts."

IT WAS THE same for the next several days. Urban slowly worked at improving and gaining more strength, while he avoided the crutches like the plague. A few weeks later, when Shane brought them over and handed them to Urban, he looked at him in horror. "Oh God no," he argued. "I really don't want to end up locked down, like last time."

"We're hoping this time it won't happen," Shane replied.

"Yeah, but you don't know that."

"No, I don't, but we do need to take this step soon. And, if you aren't ready for it, then I need to see why."

Urban hesitated.

Shane looked at him and nodded. "Remember. This isn't so much about trusting me. It's also about trusting yourself and knowing when your body will be ready for this."

"And what if I say my body isn't ready?"

"I'll ask you again if fear is holding you back or if something else is going on."

"Oh, it's fear all right, fear of agony again."

"Got it. But, at the same time, you also know that you have faced a lot of hurdles in life, and a lot of them looked to be the same kind of hurdles, but you overcame all of them anyway. And that's what you're facing now again."

"Easy to say"—Urban stared at him—"but definitely not easy to do." Still persuaded by Shane's commonsense arguments, Urban slowly positioned the crutches under his arms and maneuvered himself vertical again. Just even being upright was such an incredible feeling. He looked down at the floor. "The only thing about this is that the floor seems awfully far away."

"Only when you fall," Shane replied, with a note of humor.

He looked at him in surprise and then realized he was joking. "Oh, I hear you, but please, no *falling down* jokes," And he stiffly took one step and then another. "So is that enough?"

"Nope, we'll go out in the hallway."

He winced. "Please tell me that we're not going for a

long walk."

"No, not very long," Shane responded. "I just want to go down the hallway and back, and I want you to work on walking as close to normal as you can."

"There is no *normal* in my world right now."

"No, there isn't, but I also need to know how and what muscles you're using."

"I thought the whole problem was I wasn't using a lot of them," Urban pointed out jokingly. But his humor was an attempt at staving off the fear of what was to come. "I sure hope you know what you're doing."

"So do I," Shane agreed. "Now come on. Let's go. No more excuses."

And slowly, ever-so-slowly, using his crutches, Urban made his way down the hallway. He wasn't even struggling to go down the hallway. However, it was just more of the fear of what would happen afterward. But he made it down, and he made it back, and he smiled triumphantly at Shane. "Yet it was easier last time," he noted.

"That's because you're making it more work today because you're so afraid of ending up injured that you're not really walking normally. So, that's pulling all kinds of other muscles into effect."

"I could put the crutches to the side and just walk," he suggested, "but I'm pretty sure it would be more like a hobble or a bad crab walk."

"Give me the crutches and take a few steps toward me."

Urban handed over the crutches and then slowly took several steps toward Shane.

Shane nodded. "Better. Before it seemed that you were not even utilizing the crutches. In your head, you're making the crutches become the reason for the pain that you encountered last time," he murmured. "So again today, earlier, you were barely even using them. Okay, working off that premise, without the crutches this time, I want you to walk down and then slowly walk back, so I can take a look at how your gait is."

"Ouch," he moaned, but he took a wide slow circle around, walked down ten paces, turned, and came back again.

Shane nodded and handed back the crutches. "Good enough, now use the crutches."

"Is there any point if I just did it without crutches?"

"Yep, we don't want you to put the full strain on those legs yet," Shane explained, "at least on that left one that you're favoring so much. So, again."

And again Urban went through it. By the time he was done, Shane wanted him to do one more, and Urban shook his head. "No, I'm done. I can feel it."

"In that case, we stop," Shane agreed. "And it's almost dinnertime."

"Good, I'm hungry."

At that, Shane laughed. "You always seem to be hungry now."

"I am. I don't know what is doing that, but I'm grateful because wow. Besides, it's really good food served here." He chuckled again.

"You're right, it is. And I'm getting kinda hungry myself too."

"I don't know how you guys don't gain weight here," he muttered. And then he thought about it and added, "But you all work really hard, so maybe that's what it is."

"I think that's a lot of it," Shane agreed. "I also work out, and I work out with you guys sometimes, when it's appropriate. Depends on where your own healing level is at."

"In other words, you get a heck of a lot more exercise than I individually do."

"No, not more than you do," Shane corrected, "just that I get a lot, enough that I don't have to worry about my food intake very much. But I never really relax my focus because those pounds can creep up before you have a chance to even understand that they did."

And Urban considered that later that evening, as he sat out on the deck in the cool evening air, with a cup of hot water. Dennis had tried to offer him a cup of herb tea, but Urban's mom used to drink simply hot water, and he'd thought it was the weirdest thing, but now he just drank a cup himself. It was too late for coffee, and he didn't want any black tea, and herb tea was still something he struggled with. But, as he sat here in the cooling evening air, he heard a laugh behind him that made him smile.

When a warm hand landed on his shoulder, Bettina leaned over and asked, "Hey, how you doing?"

"I'm okay. I just wanted to get out of my room for a bit."

"Away from all that paperwork from your brother?"

He smiled. "Hey, the paperwork's coming along," he said. "It's just a case of trying to figure out what other things I might want to change, before we start signing documents."

Chapter 11

"SO YOU'LL GO ahead with working with your brother?" Bettina asked. "I have about ten minutes for a break."

Urban motioned at the chair beside him. "I'll never say no to ten minutes with you."

She plunked down beside him, a smile on her face. "Are you pretty happy with the business proposal?"

"I think so. Nothing's really decided yet, but we'll go ahead. He's looking to take some time off, and I'll start taking over a couple of his businesses, until I decide what I want to run myself."

She studied him and then raised her eyebrows. "You make it sound so simple," she murmured. "For me, that would be a huge undertaking."

"Yet, for me, it's not. Still, you can't ever really minimize what a change in life that'll be for me," he noted. "It's like finding out that you're, ... that you just had an accident and that your whole world's changed. You can't prepare for something like that. You think you can, and you think you're prepared mentally. However, when it happens, you realize that you've been fooling yourself the whole time."

"I don't know if *fooling yourself the whole time* is really what you've been doing, but obviously, who can have that awareness of what would be involved, until you are in it?

Suddenly the things that you thought you could do so easily are much harder."

Urban nodded. "It's frustrating because you think that you're doing really great, and then something so simple sets you back for a very long time."

"But it sounds like you're almost there again," she murmured.

"I am. These last couple weeks have been going much better."

"And you've been here over two months now."

He chuckled. "Every once in a while, the passage of time gets to me. Then I force myself to stop and to refocus on me and on today, instead of on my brother and what he wants tomorrow."

She gazed up at him, as she murmured, "And again, a very good insight."

He shrugged and laughed. "I do have a few things to offer, every once in a while."

"No," she countered, "you have a lot to offer. It's just sad when you don't see it yourself."

"I don't know," he murmured. "I think sometimes life is just a series of challenges, and sometimes you rise to it, and sometimes it's a little more than you thought you could handle, and it takes you out, at least temporarily. Then you have to get back up and try again because there's really no other option. It's either that or just lay down in bed until you die. I just don't know why you would ever think about doing something like that"—he grinned—"since it would be so boring. Plus, why would you stay in bed and miss out on meals?" He snorted. "I couldn't hunger strike for the life of me."

"No, not you," she agreed, with a bright smile. "You like

your groceries too much."

He nodded. "And honestly, life is a gift," he murmured. "After my original accident, things were looking pretty bleak, and I knew I was heading for a wheelchair for the rest of my life. And, more than that, it was the pain, the constant agonizing pain that made me think that it would have been better if I died. But then almost immediately I got this instant thought. *No, don't even think like that.* Because I knew that, for me, I had so much joy in just waking up in the morning and seeing the sun, smelling the fresh air around me or the scent of a rose, feeling a breeze gently touch my face. I had so many reasons to live that, even though there were a lot of reasons to give up and just as many to stop fighting any longer. However, that just wasn't me, and I had to be true to me."

"You always have to be true to you," she murmured. "I think that's so much of what we are about. It is learning to be you, instead of trying to be somebody else or to even please someone else. And this is the new you. This is the you who you get to live with for the rest of your life. And change can be tough. Adjusting to life's challenges can be hard. Nobody likes enduring these accidents and injuries, but it's there. You must deal with it. And so this is all about finding a relationship with you and your body that you can live with from now on," she murmured.

"And sometimes that's easy, and sometimes it's really hard," he admitted.

She chuckled, stood up, and said, "I always love our conversations, but I have to do rounds."

And, with that, he watched as she walked away.

She thought about his words a lot, as she finished her shift and headed off to the dining room to grab some yogurt, before heading to her apartment. She wanted a swim also and just to take some time to unwind. As her night shift went, it hadn't been bad. It had been steady, and she felt more tired than she expected.

When she walked into the dining area, she noted no parfaits were set out yet. She frowned as she studied the offerings.

When Dennis called to her, she turned to find him bringing out a big tray of them. "Oh, good," she said. "I was afraid you didn't have any this morning."

"Nope, sometimes it just takes a little longer to get them out here."

"I get it. I had a pretty busy evening too."

He nodded. "Some days are just like that, aren't they? No matter what we do, we still can't quite get ahead."

"I somehow managed to stay up with it"—she yawned—"but I am tired."

"Grab your breakfast and go get some sleep," Dennis urged.

She didn't require any further urging. Bettina grabbed a large yogurt parfait with fresh raspberries. "This one looks delicious." And she decided to take it back to her place, instead of eating on the deck. As she walked outside, she took several bites, stopping to look at the Hathaway House support bunny, Hoppers, who was already outside, enjoying the fresh air. She picked fresh grass for him, from where it was all longer against the edges of his fence, and dropped it in. He immediately hopped over and took several nibbles. "See? You don't need much to make you happy, do you?"

At that, she heard Stan saying, "That was a pretty interesting comment."

"Oh, just one of those things that you think about.

Sometimes the patients here, the people here," she corrected, "have a very unique look at life." She glanced around at the horses grazing in the distance. She pointed at them as well. "All of them do."

"I think we all do, particularly here," he agreed. "Everybody's had their life tossed up, and however it's landed has given us a whole new look at the way the world functions around us."

She smiled at him, then pointed to the bunny. "And this guy, he just seems to be happy to have grass."

"He was pretty happy to be let out this morning, and now he'll spend his day, stretching out, catching as many sun rays as he can, before finding something else to nibble on." Stan smiled. "Not a bad life, if you can do it."

"Not at all," she murmured. She yawned again.

Stan said, "Go, go. These night shifts for you guys are brutal."

"I've been doing it for so long that I'm used to it, but I know that it's not supposed to be good for us on a long-term basis. It screws up our circadian rhythms or similar things." She shrugged. "Thankfully I'm still relatively young, and I can heal from something like that pretty fast."

"Still," Stan added, "you might want to consider switching out down the road."

"Down the road I will," she confirmed, "when there's a reason to. Right now, it works." And, with a wave and another handful of grass for the rabbit, she headed back to her apartment. When she let herself in, she walked out to the small deck, collapsed in the nearest chair, and slowly ate her yogurt.

Even as she was almost done, her eyelids were closing. Normally she would have a shower, but she was just too tired. She got up and made her way to the bedroom, stripped down, and stretched out on the cool sheets and fell asleep. When she woke, she had a headache and a sniffly nose. She groaned.

"*Uh-oh,*" she muttered. She immediately picked up the phone and phoned Dani. "Hey." Then Bettina started sneezing on the phone.

"*Uh-oh,*" Dani answered. "That doesn't sound good."

"No," Bettina agreed and sneezed again. "I hate to say it, but I seem to have picked up something."

"Don't come in today," Dani warned. "With as many compromised immune systems as we have…"

"I know. I know," Bettina agreed. "I'll come and get some food later."

"Or you can ask for a delivery," Dani suggested. "You know somebody's always willing to bring you something."

"I'll see how I feel in a bit," Bettina said. "Right now I think I'll just go back to bed and crash, but I wanted you to know that I won't be there for night shift."

"No, I hear that," Danie noted. "You stay where you are and recover. I'm sure tomorrow will be much better."

"I hope so." Then Bettina sneezed yet again. "Oh my, I'm really not feeling great. I'll go back to bed." With that, she ended the call and slowly made her way back to bed.

Just as she was about to go to sleep, she thought of Urban. She quickly sent him a text, letting him know that she was sick, and then she closed her eyes and more or less passed out. She woke up several times throughout the rest of the day, and each time she felt worse and worse. By the time dinnertime rolled around, she knew that food wasn't an issue because she was done, emotionally and physically.

Whatever *this* was, running through her system, sent her

to the bathroom a little too often for comfort too. She definitely didn't want any food in her system just yet. After several attempts to stay awake for a little bit longer, she pulled on her pajamas, curled up in bed, and crashed for the full night.

By the time she woke up the next morning, she almost felt better. As she got up and slowly walked around her apartment, she realized that she was feeling better but wasn't 100 percent just yet. The thing was, she was needed at work. However, if she infected other people, it would be way worse. Deciding that she would try some food and then see how her body reacted, she headed over to the dining room. It was still early, and nobody should be there yet.

Dennis looked at her with concern.

She smiled shakily. "I'm feeling better, but …"

"You don't look it," he stated bluntly. "Grab some food and head back to bed."

"Aye, aye, cap'n," she quipped. And honestly, by the time she returned with her plate of food to her apartment, it was all she could do to get it down. Then she headed to bed and crashed yet again.

URBAN WAS SURPRISED at how long Bettina had been gone. She made it back to work several days later, and Urban had missed her every single day. He had taken the opportunity to go to the vet clinic and cuddle puppies while she'd been away. A face washing, butt wiggling event that had done so much for his mental and emotional health.

Seeing her here now, she looked a whole lot better than when she'd left. Then he hoped he did too.

Bettina smiled at him. "We can't have everyone else here getting sick because the staff didn't stay home long enough. … And, yes, I get sick leave, so it's not as if it's that much of hardship. It's more of a problem for me because I felt bad the whole time. When you get a few days to stay home, the last thing you want to do is be sick."

He nodded in commiseration. "Good point. Glad you're feeling better now."

"And I am much better. I hadn't realized even how tired I was, but I was getting worn down too, I guess."

"Because of that whole night shift thing?"

"I don't know," she murmured, "but it's also a very different pace, when you're on night shift, and I kind of like it."

"Oh, I'm not trying to tell you not to do it." Urban snorted. "It's perfect for me."

She chuckled. "I don't know about *perfect,* but it is nice to see you throughout the evenings."

"It is, indeed. … I missed you while you were gone."

"I missed you too. I missed everything. I barely ate. I think I dropped like five pounds. Dennis is already on my case."

Urban burst out laughing. "I'm sure dropping five pounds in this place is an easily remedied problem."

"You're not kidding," she murmured. "When I first got here, I was so worried about losing or gaining weight that I was always very, very cautious at mealtimes. But then I realized that I'm working all the time and that I'm just not necessarily hungry. So, if I eat when I'm hungry, then I haven't had a problem with my weight."

"I think that's often the problem anyway, isn't it?" he asked. "Just enjoy life and be careful to eat when you're hungry and to stop eating when you're full."

She nodded. "Yeah, and sometimes that seems to be a life lesson all in itself."

He chuckled. "I think everything in life is a lesson."

She nodded. "And you?" she asked. "How are you getting on?"

"I'm getting there. Still a ways to go, but I am getting there."

"I heard through the grapevine that you're making great progress."

"I'm making progress," he conceded. "I'm not sure I would go with the *great* progress yet."

She smiled. "And I don't think you're all that good at taking compliments yourself."

"It's not something I'm used to." He studied her, with a thoughtful expression.

"A lot of things here aren't what you're used to," she stated, with a firm nod. "Like compassion and understanding and patience."

"No, you're right," he agreed. "Those aren't exactly well developed in the navy or air force, or any military of any kind." He shook his head. "It's all about doing your job, fealty to the country, and making sure you're not being a baby about it."

"And it's that *being a baby* part that makes it difficult for us sometimes," Bettina noted, "because people come in here with this attitude of *oorah* and *be the best of the best.*"

He nodded. "And yet that doesn't work out so well in other settings, does it?"

"Nope, sure doesn't, because the only thing you need to be the best at out here is being yourself, and most guys look at us askance when we talk like that and just don't understand."

"No, of course not because any of that kind of talk isn't something that we're used to," he murmured.

"Which is kind of too bad in a way," she noted, "because, when you think about it, an awful lot can be said for learning more about yourself all the time."

"Maybe. I don't know." Urban shrugged. "It's … It's an odd thing to discuss."

"And how are your visits with the shrink going?" she asked.

"They are ongoing. Mostly about the business side of life."

She raised her eyebrows. "Really?"

He nodded. "Absolutely. Just my insecurities."

"Because you've always been able to fall back on your talents, haven't you?"

"If you mean my strengths, yes," he clarified, with a laugh.

She grinned. "Kind of the same thing in this instance. You knew what you could do. You knew how well you could do it, and you knew that people could rely on you to do it well. But now it's a whole new playing field, so a whole lot more that you can work from."

"And yet it shouldn't be that bad," he noted. "My baby brother knows what I'm like. I've worked with him loads before. In many ways we're two of a kind."

"Maybe that part bothers you," she suggested. "Maybe you're too much alike."

"And that's possible," he agreed. "I can't say anything's really bothering me. I'm just trying to cover all my bases before I take the plunge, trying to address any problems now that may come up later."

"And that's smart," she murmured. "Nobody expects

you to blindly jump in with both feet into something like this."

"And yet most people, I think, expect us to jump constantly into all kinds of things, whether we've had a chance to assimilate it or not. For example, I follow Shane because I trust him. So a part of me says that I can follow my brother because I trust him too."

"I like that," Bettina said. "I saw him those two times, those two days he came to visit you."

"I've certainly mentioned you to him several times. Matter of fact, he seems quite surprised that I might have met somebody here. He's just broken off with his girlfriend, so he's a bit off-kilter."

"Ah," she murmured. "That's tough when you have a breakup like that."

"I think in this case it's probably a good thing though. She was bleeding him dry."

"*Ouch.* That's not necessarily helpful for anybody."

"Nope, sure isn't," Urban agreed cheerfully. "I told him as much, but, when you're still caught up in all that pain, it doesn't really matter what people say."

"Oh, that's very true," she murmured, "and he will get over it in his own time."

"Or he won't," Urban countered. "That's his choice too."

She looked over at him, a grin on her face. "Quite the philosopher, aren't you."

He shrugged. "I can almost blame this place for that," he stated, with an eye roll. "Just think about the conversations we have here."

"And I like that part," she declared. "I like that we have deep, meaningful conversations. I like the fact that we can talk about so many things under the sun. Can you imagine what it would be like to *not* talk with other people?"

"I don't know," he muttered. "Sometimes it's almost like as if would be easier because then you can just sit in silence."

"If that's what you want, fine, but I don't think too many of us want too much silence," she murmured. "I think we want our brains pushed and new ideas tossed at us to get some feedback and responses and further thoughts and see how we're doing and what we're doing and how we feel about the universe around us and the people in it." She added, "I think people are more complex than just simple animals looking for stimulus."

"And that's one of the reasons we get along so well." Urban gave her a broad smile. "Once again it's a case of, we can see a lot of things in a very similar way."

She nodded. "And I like that too."

"Me too," he agreed, once again relieved that they had so many things to talk about.

THE NEXT DAY his baby brother popped back in again. Urban smiled up at David and asked, "Hey, how you doing?"

"I'm doing okay," David replied. "I'm just checking in on you. No pressure, just a social call."

"Oh, so no pressure to see if I've signed everything yet?" Urban asked in a teasing voice.

"No, and, if you don't want to, you don't have to," David stated. "I'm just looking for help myself and a way to get you back on your feet."

"And it's appreciated. Don't you worry," Urban said.

"I'm in the process of getting things signed."

"Good," his brother said, a bit surprised.

At that, considering it was the end of the day, Urban asked, "You want to go grab a coffee?"

"Sure. … As I look around this place, I'm wondering if I shouldn't be doing more philanthropic work and offering some charity money."

"I can tell you that an awful lot of people here could use it, if you're in a position to hand it over."

He nodded. "Brother, you have no idea how much money I have."

"All I know is you were struggling over what your fiancée was spending."

"Yeah," David agreed, "I would much rather give it to a place like this than buy her the thirteenth pair of purple sandals to match the rest in her closet that she doesn't wear."

"Right, got it," Urban noted. "So you'll spend money where it's necessary."

"And that's the way I run my businesses too," he added.

"I know for a fact that a lot of people here could use the money," Urban murmured. "Keeping us here is not a cheap prospect."

"No, I can't even imagine," David admitted, "especially if the food's good."

"You have no idea." Urban grinned. "Come on. Let's go down and grab a coffee."

Wheeling him down, David was given a tour of the upstairs. They grabbed a coffee and headed out on the deck. Urban said, "Now look over the edge there." As his brother leaned over and whistled, Urban added, "Yeah, that's where I get to spend most of my time."

"Wow, no wonder you're not in any hurry to leave."

Urban burst out laughing at that. "That's only part of the reason, but, yes, I'm here until I'm not here. And I don't know when that'll be. I don't know at what point in time they decide I'm done or whether I even get it done or if it's a case of the budget money's gone." He shook his head. "I haven't asked those kinds of questions. I'm still trying to work on healing."

"You've got what? Another month and a half, two months?"

"Something like that." Urban frowned, realizing just how short that sounded. "And when you say it like that, that sounds scary."

His brother looked over at him and shook his head. "For you, no. Dude, I can't imagine anything scaring you."

"Yeah, well, after everything I've been through, … it's funny the things that do scare me."

"Like what?" David asked, studying him.

"My future, for one," he shared, "and losing somebody I just met who's very close to me."

"Ah, this mysterious woman I only saw two times for like two seconds," David noted. "I was hoping to get to know her better, spend a bit more time with her."

"And she might be here getting coffee before she heads to her shift," Urban said. "I have no way of knowing."

"You don't keep in close touch?"

"We do and we don't. I don't want to pester her, and she knows that I have classes and workshops and workouts and therapy and psychology, *and-and-and*," he replied, with an eye roll.

"Wow, they really do run you through it, don't they?"

"Not only are we recovering from major surgeries and major traumas," Urban explained, "but most of us are facing completely new lives, trying to figure out what to do, where to go, how to do it, adapting to what our current reality is versus the reality we had hoped it would be. A lot of psychological elements are involved."

Hearing a voice behind him, he turned to see Bettina walking toward him. She had a bright smile on her face. He held out a hand, and she grabbed it.

"Hey," she greeted him. "What are you doing down here? It's not even dinnertime."

Urban turned and pointed to his visitor. "My brother is here visiting again."

Surprise lit up Bettina's face, and she reached out a hand. "Hello, glad to see you could make it back again so soon."

Urban watched his brother look at her in surprise and slowly shake her hand.

David nodded. "It's good to see him. Plus he's told me a lot about you."

She flushed. "All lies I'm sure."

"I don't think so," David argued, yet chuckled. "But, hey, sounds like you've been a major part of his life here, and I want to thank you for that."

"You don't need to thank me. He is a joy to be around." She checked her watch and winced. "And I hate to say hi and run," she began, "but I was just literally trying to grab a coffee before my shift starts. And I don't want to be late." And, with that, she scampered back inside the dining room to get her coffee and then rapidly exited the area.

"That's her?" His brother sounded dazed.

Urban frowned at him and nodded. "Yeah, that's her. Why?"

David sighed. "I guess I wasn't paying much attention to

her those first two times I briefly saw her. Not until you started talking more and more about her. Somehow I thought she would probably be fat and forty and frumpy."

Urban stared at his brother for a moment and then burst out laughing. "Good Lord, why would you expect that?"

"I don't know. I really don't know," he replied, "but you were talking about a nurse who had been here since forever."

"She has been. I think she's twenty-nine." He stopped and thought about it. "I think that's what she told me. She just came back from a conference, then she was sick, so I didn't get to see her very much in the last week," Urban added with a frown. "But she's doing much better and seems to be back to normal."

"Heck, it's almost worth getting injured if I can meet people like that here," his brother said.

"You just need to meet people who aren't after your money," Urban suggested.

"Yeah, and for that I need to not look like I have as much money," David admitted, with a smile.

"Good luck with that. You're used to the best in so many ways."

"And it's partially just that business persona. You have to dress well when you're dealing with big business, and I like to dress well," he admitted. "I like to look good."

"And that's fine," Urban said, "but you also look like money."

His brother gave him a sideways look. "Does that mean you won't look like money when you get into a partnership with me?"

"I dunno," Urban replied. "I'm not even sure what that'll look like yet, ... but I already have somebody in my life. I'm certainly not fishing for more."

"Good for you." David shared an admiring look in the direction that Bettina had disappeared. "I have to admit I'm impressed." And he reached over, patted his brother on the shoulder, and said, "Go, you."

At that, Urban just considered his situation with Bettina and shook his head. "You know that I wouldn't have met her anywhere else. This is where her heart is. It's the kind of work she does here."

"So that'll keep you close," David suggested. "I like that."

"It will, indeed because I know that to suggest she leave Hathaway House would be, … would be very hard on her."

"And you're already taking her wishes into account, just not more than you are taking your own, I hope."

"No, I'm not, but, while she has a heart and soul and a focus for her world, I know that it's important for her to stay here. However, if I'm in town, that's fine too."

"Right, it's not as if that's very far away. What is it? A fifteen-minute drive?"

He nodded. "Exactly." And then he smiled. "Or I just move in here."

David stared at him. "What do you mean?"

"She's got housing here. She's lived on the property for quite a few years now."

"Wow, they have housing here for people who work here?" He stared around, shaking his head. "These grounds are absolutely amazing," he murmured. "I can't imagine the work that went into developing a place like this."

"That would be Dani," Urban noted. "Her heart and soul that went into this place. Mostly, I believe, from the things that I've heard, because of her father. He was a veteran who was really struggling with life, and they started this place to help others like him."

"You know that those are the best businesses," his brother declared. "They come from the heart. They come from the soul. Even though they don't look like moneymakers, they provide something else on the inside for those of us who feel the need to do something like this," he murmured. He looked over at his brother. "If you want to develop something like this, we could look at that."

Urban stared at him. "I hadn't even considered that."

"Or if you want to do something that complements this," David added, "we can also look at that."

"Wow," Urban muttered. "Even if we could do something that would help people like this, that would also make me feel I am doing something to pay back."

"And that's important too," his brother agreed, "because paying back acknowledges the gratitude of what you've already received and helps you to see just how much further your life has gone because of it."

Long after his brother left, Urban considered what David had said. Urban hadn't really expected comments like that from his baby brother either. It showed a sign of the times and the changes in both their worlds that they were even verbalizing something like that. Urban loved it. It made him feel whole. It made him feel strong, and it made him feel that his life had purpose again.

He still had no clue what type of business he wanted to get into, but, with his brother's backing and verbal support, it seemed like kind of an open-ended offer right now. Obviously Urban would still have to whittle his choice of a business down a little bit and get things figured out as to what *he* wanted to do. However, it sounded as if his brother was more than willing to let Urban go in a direction that his heart told him to go.

Now if only he knew what his heart wanted to do. And it really didn't at this point. It had no clue, and that was driving him the battiest of all. He sat out here on the deck for the longest time, until the dinner bell rang, and then he headed in to get some food.

Chapter 12

SEVERAL DAYS LATER Bettina realized something was going on in Urban's mind, much more than he was sharing with her. Finally, when she wasn't sure if she should even bring it up, but it was driving her nuts, she broached the subject. "So, I'm not sure what's going on, but you seem very distant—or maybe *preoccupied* is a better word." He looked at her in surprise and then immediately apologized. She shook her head. "I'm not looking for an apology," she began. "I was just wondering if it had anything to do with me."

"No, not at all," he said. "It has something to do with what my brother mentioned."

"Oh, in what way?"

"He made me think a lot about what options I had in terms of businesses to start or to take part in. I didn't realize my brother had as much money or that apparently I have as much money as I did, or do." He shook his head, confusing his tenses in his eagerness to try and explain. "But apparently, when we were talking about how Dani had started Hathaway House, David suggested that I could do something similar, if I wanted, or something that complements this."

She stared at him in surprise and delight.

"Right? And that just opened up the whole world to

something else that I could do, and yet I don't … It's almost like it's … Now I have a big world to choose from, and I, … I don't know what to do."

"And again, do you have to sort it out right now?"

"No," he stated, shaking his head. "I know my brother well enough to understand that he sees me thinking about it and that I'll get to an answer eventually. Yet I would much rather do something that helps other people, like Dani has done, than have a store," he explained, raising his hands. "While I love electronics, and I love all kinds of stuff, but do I really want to have a computer store? No." He shook his head again. "I don't think that'll fulfill me on any level that matters."

"Got it," she murmured. "I think you were truly blessed."

"I know the money will be a huge factor."

She stopped, placed a finger over his lips, and said, "And that's not what I mean."

He stared at her. "Sorry?"

She smiled. "You're blessed because you're somebody who is thinking past what it is that you can see today. You're thinking of who you can help and what you can do that might help," she explained. "Even if you don't have any answers right now, that's not the point. The fact that you've opened up your brain to even being *more*, … to seeing more possibilities? That will make the difference—in your life and the lives of others—as you move forward."

He smiled. "And it's people like you who have helped me get here," he noted.

Her smile grew even bigger. "You know you're destined for great things."

"I don't know that I am," he argued, "and I don't really

care about fame or the like. I spent a lot of my life doing great things that nobody would ever know about," he shared, "and I can't even really talk about them now. In the military, we saved all kinds of people and stopped all kinds of wars and saved failing governments. … Nobody knows about all that, which is fine. I don't do things because of the reward."

"And that," she stated, "is what's so important. You're doing things for the right reason. And, even now, while you're sitting here pondering the ways of the world, you're trying to figure out what to do with your money."

"And not just with this money, but how to make more money," he added, "because let's face it. I still have to make a living. However, I want to do it in such a way that benefits somebody. I just don't know what way to do that."

"And I'm sure you could ask somebody here in management for advice or an ear."

"Most people would say my brother would be the best bet for that," he noted, with a laugh.

"And maybe that's true. Maybe you just need to keep talking to him. See what works out of that brain of yours, and, when you come up with an idea, toss it his way and see what he has to say."

"I just might do that." Urban nodded. "It's exciting times, and I never thought that I would ever say that again."

At that, she laughed. "And you have no idea how exciting it is to see you at this stage of life," she murmured. "It's such a great time and a great stage for you, and I'm so happy."

He looked over at her and realized that she really meant it. "You're really special, you know that?"

She shook her head. "Oh, no, no, no. We're not talking about me. We're talking about you." She asked him, "Will you stay in town?" And a kernel of worry was evident in her tone.

He nodded. "I might have to do a little bit of traveling, depending on what and where we end up with the businesses," he replied, "but I wouldn't ever ask you to move away from here."

She sat down hard. "Really?" she asked hopefully. "I was kind of worried that you would leave."

"I have to leave Hathaway House eventually," he said. "That's just a fact of life."

She nodded. "Absolutely, and you want to work toward that," she agreed. "You want to graduate from this rehab center, but what do you graduate to? That's a whole different story."

"I want to graduate to independence and to a whole new world," he declared. "A world that I'm happy in. However, I also want to be near you, and you're here. This is you. This is your life. I respect that." She smiled, and he saw tears in her eyes.

"Thank you," she whispered. "I have to admit I was worried."

"Of course you were because that's who you are, but neither did you want to say anything to me."

"No, I didn't want to affect your decision." She shrugged. "You need to make decisions of your own, and I didn't want to be an influence and bring you to a point that wasn't who you were."

"No, that won't happen." He studied the woman who was so real and honest, yet somebody he knew he could spend a lot of his time with. Just then her phone buzzed.

She winced. "I have to run." And she was up and gone.

URBAN REALIZED JUST how much he loved having Bettina here, how much he loved being somebody she talked to. And maybe she talked to other patients all the time too. He didn't want to take that away from them either. So Urban would need somewhere locally as his base. And that meant he would need a place to live, and a nice place to live. If he had the money, that is.

His brother had stressed how Urban had money, but he hadn't really seen any figures, didn't know what that meant yet. But there was hopefully time, as he still had a month or two here at Hathaway House. Yet, as he thought about it, a month or two was not very long at all. Just long enough to heal, he hoped. And maybe he had enough money to stay longer, if his benefits didn't let him stay anymore.

It's funny how he hadn't even thought about money before because, well, he hadn't even considered what his future was, where he was going, or what he would be doing. And now he was considering what he could do with that money, where could it take him, and what he could create that other people needed.

And maybe that was a conversation for Dani; he didn't know. But maybe, just maybe, when he was a little bit further down this pathway, he could ask her some questions about that and what other veterans might need. Something to consider in the days to come.

Chapter 13

SEVERAL DAYS LATER Bettina broached Urban again about the subject of choosing a business to make him fulfilled. "Did you get any further on that?"

"No," he said, gasping for breath, in the wheelchair again, slowly moving down the hallway to his room. "Shane has been working my butt to the wall." He glared at Shane's retreating back. "Are you just coming on shift?" Urban asked Bettina.

"Yeah, I'm a little early," she said. "I just thought I'd pop in and see if you wanted to have a cold drink out on the deck."

"Absolutely. Anything to forget that last session."

"Yet you seem so much stronger."

"And I am," he confirmed, "no doubt about it. Stronger and doing much better, but still every day seems, in some ways, a bigger struggle."

"I don't think that ever goes away," she noted, "even when you're back to perfect health. I'm not sure that that will be something that you can really stop."

"I wonder," he murmured. "I was kinda hoping it would be better than this though."

"Maybe, but maybe not."

"Are you okay if I'm not better than this?" he asked. "What if I have days in wheelchairs?"

She frowned at him. "So? So what if you have days in wheelchairs? Do you really think that will make a difference to me?"

He smirked. "The good thing is, you're used to people in wheelchairs."

"I absolutely am." She chuckled. "Still, I'm not so shallow as to be worried about it either."

"Good," he murmured. As he slowly headed out onto the deck, he suggested, "Instead of a cold drink, how about ice cream?"

"Oh, I just might snag something like that for us," she said, with a huge smile. And she turned and headed back toward the kitchen area. Soon Bettina returned with another woman, carrying two large cones.

Urban nodded at her. "Hey, I know I've met you before, but sorry. I don't remember your name."

"That's fine," she replied. "I tend to hide in the background."

Bettina made the introductions. "This is Ilse. She's the head chef for the kitchen."

Urban frowned. "I didn't mean to have you wait on us."

"Why not?" she asked, with a note of amusement in her tone. "It is what I do here."

Urban added, "Usually Dennis is out here."

"Yep, usually Dennis would be," Ilse shared, "but he's in the kitchen, working away. I was out in the dining area for a few minutes, so believe me. I'm perfectly capable of getting you an ice cream." They both thanked her, as she turned and walked away.

Urban frowned as he watched Ilse return to the kitchen. Then he asked Bettina, "I wonder what the food services industry's needs are for places such as this."

"I imagine it's brutal," she replied. "Tons of food required on a daily basis, the logistics of getting fresh deliveries in all the time. I don't know what all is involved. Why?"

"Just thinking about the business end."

She stopped, looked at him, and chuckled. "Okay then, you're thinking of opening a food services company?"

"I have no idea," he admitted. "And, of course, opening one versus buying one, that's a different story too."

"I can't even imagine what kind of dollar figures that would require." It was mind-boggling.

"Me either," Urban noted. "It's just one of those ideas that popped up."

"Keep them popping," she said. "I'm sure there'll be something that will feel right before too long."

"Lots feels right," he noted. "Just … nothing feels *perfect*."

At that, she slowly lowered her ice cream, studying him, and asked, "Do you really expect *perfect*?"

He stared at her. "Expect? No. You're right, I guess. Still, I was thinking I wanted something that would stick around long enough, so that it wouldn't end up feeling like a passing fancy."

"Now that," she said, "I can understand. But if you're looking for perfect, that just doesn't exist. So maybe something that's better than good and something that feels right. Maybe that would be a better way to judge."

"I like that," he agreed. "*Feels right* would be *perfect*."

At that, she laughed. "So there you go, back to *perfect* again."

He chuckled. "Hey, I'll go for gold. If I go, I'll go for as far and as powerful as I can be."

"You go for it," she said. "I'm totally content to be

here."

"And I want that too," he shared. "I want that for myself."

She nodded. "I get that, and I'm not at all sure that it's a problem."

"I hope not," he stated. "I think so many possibilities are out there, and I'm just grateful for finally having access to even the thought of it. I don't believe I would have gotten there if I hadn't been here all this time."

"Maybe not," she replied, with a gentle smile, "but you're here now, and that's what counts."

THE WORD *PERFECTION* sat in the back of Urban's brain and bugged him. He didn't want to be that guy. That guy who wasn't happy until he hit perfection, that guy who wasn't happy with a project or a goal or whatever it was until it was perfection. He didn't think he was that guy, but something that Bettina had said made him wonder. Was he even close to being that guy? Was it even possible to *not* be that guy? Was life such a difficult thing in his world that he could only see the very best in his world, and he couldn't see the others?

When she questioned him a few days later, he frowned at her, shrugged, and replied, "Everybody here always makes me think deeper than what I was expecting. … I know it sounds foolish, but you mentioned *perfect*, seeking perfection."

She stared at him. "I did mention not worrying about perfection or going after perfection."

He nodded. "And I was thinking how much I don't

want to be that guy. That guy who looks at something and says, *Oh, it's terrible. I could do much better.*"

She chuckled. "I dunno. I think part of that's self-confidence."

"Maybe," he conceded. "I feel as if I'm holding off on so much in my life because I'm not good enough yet."

At that, she stopped and stared. "Now that's interesting because *not good enough* means reaching for more, where something is lacking. Therefore, you're then expecting yourself to be better at it."

"Right, and, of course, I will get better, but I don't know how much better."

"And because you don't know *how much better,* you don't know if and when you'll ever achieve whatever it is that you're looking to achieve," she pointed out, with a nod. "So definitely *not* something you want to be working on."

He stared at her and then smiled. "I get that. I just hadn't really seen it happening."

"I'm not sure if it was happening or whether it's one of those ingrained kind of things," she explained, "where it's almost a habit. You expect a certain something from someone, and, when it doesn't get there, you're not sure what to think about it. And so you fall back on the same old things that you used to process with."

"And in that case," he added, "I think it would be a case of it's not good enough, and I need to get better at it, before I move in that direction."

"Which is also interesting because how do you ever get good at something like that?" she asked in wonder.

"I have to heal *first,* so I keep putting everything off *until then.* Even with my brother, I keep thinking that, although I've verbally said yes to going into business with him, I haven't really looked at the businesses because I keep thinking, *Well, I can't do that yet. I better wait until I'm better.* But then it's not about *better.* It's not *until I'm perfect.* Plus, is there no perfect out there?"

She looked over at him, her lips twitching, and she murmured, "I don't think there is any perfect in your world because I think you'll always look at how you can make anything better. Even something already deemed *perfect.*"

He chuckled. "Maybe. … I'm feeling a little bit foolish though."

"Oh, don't do that," she said. "I think you've been doing an absolutely incredible job."

"But then the people here are all doing an incredible job. Because everybody here is already only capable of doing so much," he argued. "However, if you compare what I was doing to the real world—or to the bigger world, let me put it that way," he explained, "I don't think you'd be saying that."

She leaned over, grabbed his hands, and declared, "I think I would. I think you've been doing an incredible job, and I don't care whether you're here or you're somewhere else. The challenges that you had to face and the things that you had to deal with are phenomenal," she stated. "They're huge. They're life-altering, gobsmacking, massive, and you've done an incredible job handling all that. No, you're not *there* yet. No, you're not *perfect.* Maybe you'll never get perfect. I would hope not, as that would be an incredibly boring place to be. You don't want perfection in your life. You want something that's changeable, mutable, something that you can look up to and smile at."

He stared at her. And everything she was saying was very much something he wanted to hear, and, at the same time, he was afraid to believe it. "Are you serious?" he finally asked.

Her eyebrows popped up. "Of course I'm serious." And then she shook her head. "Or do you really think I'm just saying something like that to make you feel better?"

He gave her a quirk of his lips. "It's just that fear speaking, saying that because somebody cares for you they tell you the good things, but they don't really mean it."

"I would hope that wasn't the case," she replied. "I get that sometimes you don't want to necessarily tell the truth to somebody if it's bad news. What's that comment about *Honey, does this dress make me look fat?*" She had to laugh.

He nodded. "Kind of, but you also know what it's like when you have a mother who's got a child who brings home this art piece, which is absolutely terrible, but you tell him for encouragement's sake that it's absolutely wonderful."

She smiled. "Let me start with this. What you and I have is special. And what we have is something that we are learning to live with and to adapt to and to change with and to grow with," she shared, reaching for one of his hands. "But I would also want it to be based on trust and truth. And if it is an issue that matters, I want you to know that I will give you as honest and as clear and as concise an answer as I can. Sure, maybe I won't like everything in life, and maybe I won't have the right answer for you to every question. Some days I'll say the absolute wrong thing," she stated, "but you have to know that I'm coming from the heart and that I'm not trying to hurt you. And right now I think you just need to have a little more self-confidence in who you are and in what you're doing and in where you're going. Maybe you just need to be good with the fact that you don't know all those answers beforehand."

He chuckled. "You're right again. This is definitely one

of those times where I do feel as if everybody here is way ahead of the curve than I am."

"It's not that we're ahead of the curve," she argued, "but we definitely have seen things over and over again, and that gives us a completely different perspective than what you might expect. And if you aren't looking at it from the same point of view that we are, our information comes across as different."

He nodded and smiled at her. "I get that. As long as you can give me as much of an honest answer as you can and not treat me like a two-year-old, we should be good."

At that, she burst out laughing. "I don't see you as a child in any way, shape, or form," she stated firmly. "And I want to know that we can at least trust each other to that extent. I wouldn't want to have a relationship where I felt somebody was giving me answers he thought I *wanted* to hear instead of the answers that I *needed* to hear. So, when I ask you a question, I want to hear your honest answer."

"Got it," he said and gave her a cheeky grin. "So you feel the same way I do, *huh?*"

"I hope so," she hedged, looking at him with a smile. "And every time it seems like we go forward a little bit and back a little bit."

"But," he noted, "we're inching in the right direction every time."

"That we are." She chuckled. "I can't argue with that."

"Good. I really don't want to argue. Today's been a long day."

She looked at him quizzically.

He shrugged. "Just one of those visits with the shrink, where you wonder if you're doing everything that you can to move forward in life. Then, because you ask some question, she asked a few more questions, which leads to more questions, and—before you know it—you're not sure that you've done anything right and, with so much more ahead of you, that you'll never get there."

"Ah. I imagine that these people play a very valuable role in what they do, but I can also see that from the other side. It seems to be a never-ending road, and it never gets any better, and, as you take a step forward, you also then take a step back."

"And when you take a step back," he pointed out, with a smile, "it's really another five or six steps back. And you lose sight of what's supposed to be progress. Instead all you can see is the negative of how far you haven't come."

"I think that's where the danger lies, when you get hung up on that negative side," she said sadly. "Depression is an all-too-common occurrence here, and it's not just for people who are doing poorly. It's also for people who are doing well. A lot of people are scared of success. A lot of people are scared of what comes after they become a success because then the onus is on them to pick up the pieces of their life and to move forward. And it's a scary thought. Who wants to move forward, when, in your mind, you're still a broken-down body not capable of handling what's out there? Or still afraid of people's reactions to seeing you?"

She shook her head and continued. "That's not you—at least not that I'm still seeing—and I'm grateful it's not you. However, if it were you, it would be something that we would deal with. It's not something that we must have answers for. It's something that you learn to move forward with." She got up and said, "I'll be back in a little bit. You okay for now?"

He smiled. "I'm always okay."

Chapter 14

B ETTINA NODDED AT Urban. "That's one of the things I like about you," she said. "Even when you're not okay, you always try to be okay." And, with those cryptic words, she took off. She wasn't sure whether or not she was getting the message across in the way she wanted to.

It was a little confusing for her to deal with some of these issues because Urban really was going forward and then backward. But, as she thought about what he noted from the shrink's visit, that made a lot of sense. She just had never considered it or seen it at this level. But then she didn't deal with the patients at this level. She didn't deal with them long-term or in any way that seemed to impact their conversations. She saw them on a superficial level.

This deep-level interaction she only had with him. Urban. This was her first experience at this level. And it was confusing. She wasn't sure how to handle it or if she was even handling it properly. She wondered if she should mention it to somebody and then realized that in a way that felt like a betrayal of trust. And that she didn't feel comfortable with.

Still, several days passed before she brought this up again. She walked over to Urban before her shift and after he was done with his day. He was sitting on the side of his bed, staring aimlessly around.

"Hey," she greeted him, after he answered her knock. "How's your day been?"

"Rough," he admitted, giving her a lopsided grin, "but then lots of the days here are rough."

"Sorry," she whispered.

He shrugged. "It is what it is. You just coming to work?"

She nodded. "And what are you doing?"

"I'm heading to the pool," he said instantly. "I'm really beat, and I need to decompress today."

"Was it hard physically with Shane or with the shrink?"

"Actually I got hit with both today." He shook his head. "Literally a confusing day."

"Sounds like the pool then," she agreed. "If you want to go on down, I'll get you a coffee or something to go with it."

He stared at her. "That's not a bad idea," he muttered, "but I hate to have you running around and delivering things for me."

"We've been over that." She grinned. "Some of the things that I'm allowed to do is look after patients."

"Right," he said. "Why don't you give me, say, an hour down there and let me get some of that energy burnt off and then maybe something like that would be lovely. Especially if you have a moment to spend it with me."

"I can only spend so much time with you," she noted. "I keep expecting somebody to lower the boom on me and tell me that I'm spending too much time with you."

He stared at her. "I wouldn't want to get you in trouble."

"And I don't think it would get me in trouble," she clarified. "I think, at the very worst, I'd get a warning about remembering that I was on payroll."

"And I'm a bad one for that too," he said. "It's just so

nice to spend time with you that I tend to forget that you're working."

"I get that," she agreed, with a laugh, "because I'm bad that way too."

When she was gone, she quickly headed back to work, thinking about his words. She hadn't really thought about it, but maybe it was an issue. And should she nip it in the bud before it became an issue or just let it ride and see if anybody said anything? She was still pondering it when she completed her rounds, which returned her to her office. It was almost time to go and check on him.

Dani poked her head in the nurses' station. "Everything okay?"

"Yeah," Bettina replied. "I was just wondering if people were irritated if I'm spending too much time with Urban. I just finished my rounds, and he's in the pool, working out after a tough day," she explained. "I was seeing about delivering him a coffee at the pool. Then it occurred to me that maybe I'm pushing my limits here, maybe I'm upsetting people."

Dani frowned at her. "So, is that your own fears maybe?"

"Maybe. I'm also just very aware that I am spending a lot of time with him, and that's probably not kosher."

"I haven't heard any complaints from anybody on either side of that," Dani replied, with a smile. "So thanks for considering it. Keep it in mind that you are on payroll and that you have way more than just him to look after, but, if you have time in your schedule to deliver a coffee for him, then by all means take him coffee. You know we're all about customer care here."

"I know," Bettina agreed. "I just … It was funny because I mentioned it to him, and he was really worried that I would get into trouble. And I didn't think so, but, as I was sitting here, I wondered if I just didn't know that I was getting into trouble because nobody mentioned anything."

"I would try to nip something like that before it got to the point where you were in trouble," Dani shared, "but honestly, nobody has complained to me about it."

"That's good," Bettina replied.

"As long as you're worried about it," Dani added, "chances are you haven't crossed the line in any way."

"You always worry though," Bettina added.

At that, Dani chuckled. "And because you're worried is how I know that it's probably completely fine. And, if it ever came to that, I would say something." She turned to leave but stopped to ask, "How are you two doing?"

"Good. He's in a state of one day forward, one day back. There's progress, no progress. He's depressed, not depressed." She shrugged. "Sometimes I don't really know how he is."

"And I think that's probably pretty normal for most of them," Dani noted, with a nod. "You know they have an awful lot of progress, then suddenly they plateau, and they can't understand why. So they've been at the heights of euphoria because they can see it, and then they're at the depths of depression because they're absolutely positive that it will never get any better."

She chuckled. "Yes, I hear that. I wanted to mention it to somebody as to whether that was normal or not."

"It is, indeed," Dani declared. "How are the two of you, as in your relationship?"

"Still going strong," Bettina said cheerfully. "Although sometimes I do wonder when I hear the forward and back. He's never really made the relationship part of that forward and back process, but I know it could be."

"The way to stop that is to communicate."

"I guess, but, as long as things are moving forward, I don't really feel as if I want to rock the boat."

"No, but it would stop the insecurity."

"I don't feel insecure," she noted. "I feel pretty strong about it."

"Good," Dani replied. "Then you're right. No point in bringing it up. You'll just potentially cause more confusion."

"Maybe," she muttered. But now that Dani had put that idea in Bettina's head, Bettina noted that she and Urban had talked lots but hadn't really made decisions. As she delivered his coffee, she sat down on the side of the hot tub and faced him. "So just for clarity's sake," she murmured, "I just want to ask if we really are on the same page as far as relationships."

He paddled closer. "I thought so," he said, his gaze searching her. "Is there a problem?"

"No, no." She shook her head. "I just had a talk with Dani today about whether the work was a problem or not. Whether I was spending too much time with you or whether anybody had complained."

"And?" he asked. "Was she upset?"

"No, she wasn't at all." Bettina smiled. "And that's kind of what I expected, but I felt better after talking to her. And she's the one who asked me about our relationship, and I told her that we were doing really well. And she asked me if we were on the same page about where we're going, and I said yes, we were. She thought that was good because, if you're not, then confusion and doubt can set in. And it just kind of left me standing at that spot, saying, *Hey, I think we're on the same page, know where we're going.* Plus I'm generally not somebody who jumps into *relationship* conversations, just because they can be awkward and disconcerting."

"Yeah, they can be," he agreed, "but, as we discussed already, we would always be honest."

"And I appreciate that, so …" She stopped, feeling foolish.

"So? … So what exactly? So are we on the same page? Is that what you're trying to get at?"

"Yeah," she said. "Again, everything's fine until somebody brings up another point."

"And that's what I go through every day in therapy," he noted. "Everything's fine. I go in there feeling great, and then I come out, wondering if I have any awareness of what's going on in my world at all because, by the time I'm done in there, I'm usually pretty racked up with insecurity, guilt, or something."

"Got it," she murmured.

"It's funny, isn't it? We're fine as long as we don't discuss it, but the minute you come up for discussions on some of this stuff, you realize you're really not fine. And even though you thought you were fine, if you can't answer the questions when they're asked, they just create more doubt." He added, "Even when you can answer the questions, afterward it's like an insidious little bit of you that's saying, *Hey, I think I know what's going on, but are we really there?*"

She nodded. Just then her phone buzzed. "Oops, have to go. Think about what I said, will you?" And, with that, she bolted.

URBAN HAD ALREADY thought about it many, many times, and, like her, he'd figured that they were on the same page and hadn't really questioned it. However, now that she'd brought it up, he realized that they hadn't discussed anything outside of the fact that they really liked each other. They'd skirted the core issues—love and marriage. He groaned as he thought about it. That was hardly fair, and he didn't want in any way to keep her on a hook like that.

However, he was the one feeling insecure about taking a step forward because he didn't have, as far as he was concerned, a full life to offer. He certainly knew that he was getting better and stronger, and he used the wheelchair as rarely as possible. Plus, he was walking a little bit more every time. But he hadn't made a big scene out of it. As the days went by, he worked with Shane more and more to get his balance and to walk with better posture and to sit for longer periods.

So, when he walked in with Shane to dinner on a Friday night a few days later, he had a big grin on his face.

Dennis took one look and started to hoot and holler. "Lookie here," he crowed. "Now if that isn't a sight for sore eyes."

And Urban realized just how much he'd been waiting for this moment. And it wasn't perfect. It wasn't even close, but it was that progress in his head that he needed. That … That knowledge that he could be this advanced from where he'd been so long ago, that the surgeries that had held him back all this time had worked, and here he was in an incredible position of walking in for a meal on his own.

He stared at Shane and said, "I owe you for this."

"No," Shane disagreed. "You owe me nothing."

"I couldn't have done it without you," Urban argued.

"And I couldn't have done it without you," Shane stated, quirking his lips at him. "Remember? It's a two-person job."

"You're right." Urban stopped and frowned. "You know what? It's not even a two-person job. It's an entire community."

At that, Shane laughed. "Now you're getting it. From Dennis here, who feeds you and makes sure that your nutrients are topped right up, so that we have something to work with, to the nurses, who look after you all night long, it really is a team effort."

"I knew that on an abstract level, but I hadn't *seen* that."

"And now," Shane declared, "that paradigm shift will make a big improvement in your own view of the world around you."

"I think just getting back on my feet every day will do that," he stated, with a bright smile.

And just behind him he heard somebody else call out.

"Whoa, am I seeing what I'm seeing?"

And, sure enough, Bettina stood in shock, a huge grin of joy on her face. She raced toward him, and he grabbed hold of one of the support bars at the buffet, just in case she was about to throw herself at him. Almost as if she realized that she could knock him off his feet, at the last minute, she skidded to a stop and then gave him the gentlest of hugs. He chuckled, as he wrapped his arms around her and held her close.

"I was afraid you would run into me and knock me over," he admitted. "Even with all my progress, I would've fallen flat on my face."

She stepped back, and he could see the sheen of tears in her eyes.

"It's been a very interesting journey," he told her. "I finally realized just how much of it is all team effort, not just Shane here, not just Dani putting this together, but also ..." He looked over at Dennis and nodded. "Dennis and Ilse, the kitchen help, the office assistants, the ice cream and the food, just keeping the morale up all the time," he murmured. "Just so much goes into this place."

"There is, indeed," Shane concurred at his side. And he added, "And, while you're taking up all the space, I'll step around you and get my dinner. And if you're unlucky," he stated, "it'll be gone before you get there."

Turning slowly and making sure to keep his balance solid and on firm footing, he stepped up behind Shane and stated, "Now that's cheating."

"It is, indeed," Shane concurred. "But, hey, you got a girlfriend at your side, whereas I'm trying to rush over and meet my partner."

At that they then good-naturedly teased Shane, as he raced off to meet up with Melissa.

Urban stepped up to Dennis. "Hit me with whatever you got," Urban said. "I'm super hungry, and, after today, I feel as if all this has a big purpose."

"It sure does," Dennis declared, as he handed him a rack of ribs and a potato dish, and a big Greek salad.

"Oh my God," Urban noted, "ribs."

"Yep, ribs." Dennis chuckled. "Always good food here, you know that."

"I do know that," Urban stated, "but some food? Well, they're just *gooder* than others."

At that, Dennis burst out laughing. "I hear that sentiment a lot. Believe me. Ribs are a very popular dinner here."

"Is that why Shane raced ahead?" Urban asked Dennis.

"Oh, absolutely," Dennis replied. "I hate to say it, but

we have on occasion run out of ribs."

Urban stared at his plate and looked over at the ribs on the buffet still and asked, "Don't suppose I can get another one or two of those then, *huh?*"

Still chuckling, Dennis cut one slab in half and added it to his plate. "I doubt you can eat more than that," he noted, "but let me know."

Urban nodded. "I'll convince Bettina to get an extra couple pieces, just in case," he teased.

"Oh, I'll get a couple extra ribs," she declared, "but watch out because I'll eat them too." And, with all the camaraderie, they headed out to the deck. She noted, "It's overcast today, and it's a little bit cooler. You want to try outside?"

"I absolutely want to try outside," Urban stated. And feeling a success like he hadn't felt in a long time, he was emboldened to put his tray down and walk back over to get his cutlery and to bring two bottles of water. She sat here watching. "You know this is the first time," he said.

"First time for what?" she asked curiously.

"That I got to bring you something," he declared, with a huge smile, as he handed her a bottle of water.

She looked at it in delight. "Progress," she stated. "Doesn't it feel great?"

"It's more than great," Urban clarified as he gaze wandered the beautiful setting outside. Horses grazing. A dog wandering along a pathway – a three legged dog at that. Even… a young llama… Bringing his gaze back to her loving features he added, "It's incredible. Absolutely incredible."

Chapter 15

Aﬀer dinner Bettina had to race back to work again. She left Urban with a gentle pat on his shoulder, and this time she felt almost a tearing loneliness at having to leave him. To see him like he was, to see how proud he was of being able to get her a bottle of water, and just to see the man on his feet? It was a triumph that she wasn't quite willing to separate from. But she had work to do, and that was why she was here, and she loved every moment of it and didn't want to jeopardize any of it.

By the time she had her next break, she walked to his room. She knocked on his door, and, when he called out to come in, she found him tucked into bed. "Hey, bedtime already?"

He nodded. "I don't want to push it, and I am tired."

"Hey, that was a lot today. I just wanted to stop in to tell you how proud I am of you."

He looked up at her, and he let out a slow deep breath. "You know that you were the best thing for me that I have met or had in my life in a very long time."

"And that is a lovely thing to say."

"And I mean it. I'm not just saying it. I mean it. And I wanted … I was thinking back to what you told me to think about."

She felt her stomach clenching. "Right, about us."

"Yes, about us, and I, … I know I was kind of holding off and hemming and hawing about it all. Because, of course, we have something very special, and we are heading toward a very unique future." He took a deep breath. "I just … I don't know why I was holding back mentally, more so because I wasn't sure how I would progress physically. And I was dealing with lots of insecurities about my injuries, my appearance. Even if you weren't." The last bit he added in such a wry tone she didn't know what to say.

She hitched up a hip and sat down on the side of the bed beside him. "And?" she prompted, when he didn't say anything more.

He gave her a lopsided grin. "And"—he gave her a brief smile—"I don't have a viable job yet. I don't even have a hard-working, self-employed business of my own yet. … However, I just wanted to know if …" And then he hesitated again.

"If what?" she asked. She unscrewed the bottle of water that she had, tilted her head back, and had a long sip as she waited for him.

"I just wanted to know if …" Then he took a deep breath, and the words just poured out of him. "If you'd marry me."

She choked on the water, so shocked at his comment that, when she finally cleared her throat from choking, she stared at him wordlessly.

"I am not sure that that's a good answer." Urban stared at her warily.

"Oh my." She shook her head.

"Oh." He frowned.

Such a dark note filled his tone that she realized shaking her head had been an instinctive reaction on her part but not what her response was. So she immediately reached out and clarified, "No, no, I don't … I don't mean that."

"What do you mean then?" he asked, looking at her in confusion.

"You shocked me, as if almost choking to death didn't tell you that." She laughed. "And it's not that I was shocked about the subject matter. I was just shocked about the fact that you are taking it to this level right now."

"That's because I love you," he said. "It took me a while to figure it out, but then today I could see it clearly. And I realized everything I've been working for hadn't been for *my* future. I'd been working for *your* future, so that I could ask that question, so that I could offer it to you as a strong, healthy adult male." He took a deep breath. "I can't say that your response is exactly the response I was hoping for, though."

"Of course not," she said, with a gentle smile. "I do have an answer for you." He waited, one eyebrow raised, and she murmured, "The answer is yes."

He stared at her in his own shock. "Really?"

"Yes," she repeated, still laughing. "Really. And your injuries, your appearance as you put it? I know someone special when I see him."

"Seriously?" he asked again, as if in doubt.

She chuckled. "Absolutely." She leaned over to kiss him on the cheek, but he tightly hugged her and brought her beside him on the bed. She squealed in laughter.

When Shane's head poked around the door, he frowned at them.

She chuckled. "I'm fine. Yes, I was squealing, but I have a reason."

"What's that?" Shane asked, his gaze going from one to

the other.

"He just asked me to marry him," she shared, with a huge grin on her face.

Shane stared at them and then bounded forward. "Seriously?"

She nodded, laughing as Shane picked her up off the bed, swung her around, and then carefully deposited her back down again. "Now that," he said, "is awesome news." And he reached out a hand and high-fived Urban. "Talk about way to go, buddy."

"I know," Urban agreed. "I wasn't sure I'd get there but, because of you and because of that whole team involved, I did. And I can't be happier."

With Shane's congratulations still ringing in Urban's ears, Shane quickly disappeared down the hallway to spread the news.

She looked over at him. "You know that now we'll be inundated."

"Yep." He gave her a beaming smile. "And I don't care." And he reached out, snagged her up in his arms, held her close against his heart, and whispered, "I was too afraid to hope."

"*Our future*. That's what you were working toward, and so was I. So how *perfect* that we'll get exactly what we were hoping for."

He looked over at her, smiled, tilted her chin ever-so-slightly for a better angle, leaned in closer, and whispered, "To us." And kissed her gently.

Epilogue

V ICTOR WESTRIDGE STUDIED the website. He'd heard so much about this place that it was becoming the best-known secret around. But he'd applied a long time ago and hadn't heard. And then, all of a sudden, out of the blue, he'd gotten a response, and now he had paperwork to fill out, if he was still interested. He was still interested, already, but can you believe it?

As he looked at the computer screen and saw the glowing accolades, he wondered if it was even possible. Could something be that good? He wasn't so sure. And yet he knew several people who had been there and had made it through rehab, and he still wasn't exactly sure if they were all lying and making this up or what.

Just then one of the VA nurses, Gerry, walked in to check his blood pressure. Something that he was constantly being hit with. From beside his bed, she glanced at the website casually and said, "Oh, now look at that. That's a place for you to get in to, if you can."

"Why is that?" he asked her.

"I've heard nothing but great things about it," she told him. "And I have had previous patients contact me afterward, telling me what an absolute delight it was to go there. If you get a chance, go."

"I just got an acceptance," he shared, with a wry look,

"but I don't know if my doctors will let me travel."

"Your blood pressure's high, and we do have some problems stabilizing some of your medications," she noted, as she looked down at his stump. "And it depends on the healing on that leg."

"You mean, on the lack of a leg," he clarified, looking down.

She nodded. "It's pretty fresh, and you have a long way to go in that healing department. But they would help you a lot." She added, "You also lost three-quarters of a buttock, and that's something else to be of concern."

"Meaning the fact that I won't sit much."

"Or ever," she noted. "If these guys take you on, give them a shot. They'll do an awful lot more for you there than we can here. Here they've done the rough work, but that special physio is what you need next." She shook her head. "I don't know that you can get what you need here."

"They've got a ton of paperwork for me to deal with," he complained, "and that's kind of next on my list."

"Do it," she urged. "And let me know how you make out."

"I can try. Do you know anybody who works there?"

"Yes, one of my friends works in the kitchen."

"Yeah? As a cook?"

"She's a line cook or something like that. She works for somebody named Dennis."

"Interesting. You can always let her know that I might be coming."

"I tell you what," Gerry suggested. "You fill out your paperwork, and I'll tell her that you're coming. When you get there, you tell her that I sent you."

He chuckled. "In other words, you just want the credit

for me going."

"I would love to have the credit for you going," she admitted. "I know it would be a great place."

"So why are you still here?"

"Because they don't have staff turnover," she shared. "Otherwise I would be there in a heartbeat."

"I can always put in a good word for you too."

She stared at Victor in surprise. "Now that's a deal, and thank you for that."

He shook his head. "You've looked after me for how many months now?" he began, "and very selflessly too. So I have no problem recommending you for work there."

"Good, I would absolutely love to end up there. However, in the meantime, we have to get you there first."

"Okay, I got another deal." He grinned. "I'll get this application in and completed, if you can help me with this mess of paperwork I have to fill out."

She burst out laughing. "It's a deal. I'll come back on my coffee break." And, with that, she disappeared.

And he stared down at the website, grinning. "Maybe it is my lucky day after all," he murmured to himself. "If Gerry's willing to go to bat to get me there, maybe there's something to be said for this Hathaway House place."

He could hope so. It seemed as if he'd come as far as he could here, and, even now, as he stared down at the mangled end of his stump, it wasn't looking great. He probably couldn't travel for a while, but he sure wanted to. Anything to get out of here, anything to get away from the memories. Yet the thought of the trip was enough to make his blood curdle too. But, hey, change didn't come without pain, and he was prepared for pain—if it meant improvements.

So he opened up the forms again. And winced. "I'll be

here all night," he muttered. But there was no time like the present to get started, so he got down to work, grabbed a pen, and started getting the information together that he needed to fill out these forms. Hopefully this would be the change that he needed in his life. Now and forever.

This concludes Book 21 of Hathaway House: Urban.
Read about Victor: Hathaway House, Book 22

Hathaway House: Victor
(Book #22)

Welcome to Hathaway House. Rehab Center. Safe Haven. Second chance at life and love.

Victor found it hard to stay upbeat when faced with a life of pain and a body that seemed more broken than whole. Adding to his depression is that his injuries were deliberately caused by "friendly fire" during a joint training session. It was hard to feel his way through the fog, until one of his therapy sessions brought up the concept of finding joy in his life.

As a pastry chef, Dawn loves to play with food. It makes her happy to see others smile. Only in Victor's case the smiles were far between and too few to count. She made it her mission to find little ways to make him smile—only to realize that she was far too attached, considering he'd be leaving soon.

Can he find a way forward, without leaving her behind?

Find Book 22 here!

To find out more visit Dale Mayer's website.

https://geni.us/DMSVictor

Author's Note

Thank you for reading Urban: Hathaway House, Book 21! If you enjoyed the book, please take a moment and leave a short review.

Dear reader,

I love to hear from readers, and you can contact me at my website: www.dalemayer.com or at my Facebook author page. To be informed of new releases and special offers, sign up for my newsletter or follow me on BookBub. And if you are interested in joining Dale Mayer's Reader Group, here is the Facebook sign up page.
http://geni.us/DaleMayerFBGroup

Cheers,
Dale Mayer

About the Author

Dale Mayer is a *USA Today* best-selling author, best known for her SEALs military romances, her Psychic Visions series, and her Lovely Lethal Garden cozy series. Her contemporary romances are raw and full of passion and emotion (Broken But … Mending, Hathaway House series). Her thrillers will keep you guessing (Kate Morgan, By Death series), and her romantic comedies will keep you giggling (*It's a Dog's Life*, a stand-alone novella; and the Broken Protocols series, starring Charming Marvin, the cat).

Dale honors the stories that come to her—and some of them are crazy, break all the rules and cross multiple genres!

To go with her fiction, she also writes nonfiction in many different fields, with books available on résumé writing, companion gardening, and the US mortgage system. All her books are available in print and ebook format.

Connect with Dale Mayer Online

Dale's Website – www.dalemayer.com
Twitter – @DaleMayer
Facebook Page – geni.us/DaleMayerFBFanPage
Facebook Group – geni.us/DaleMayerFBGroup
BookBub – geni.us/DaleMayerBookbub
Instagram – geni.us/DaleMayerInstagram
Goodreads – geni.us/DaleMayerGoodreads
Newsletter – geni.us/DaleNews

Also by Dale Mayer

Published Adult Books:

Shadow Recon
Magnus, Book 1
Rogan, Book 2
Egan, Book 3
Barret, Book 4
Whalen, Book 5
Nikolai, Book 6

Bullard's Battle
Ryland's Reach, Book 1
Cain's Cross, Book 2
Eton's Escape, Book 3
Garret's Gambit, Book 4
Kano's Keep, Book 5
Fallon's Flaw, Book 6
Quinn's Quest, Book 7
Bullard's Beauty, Book 8
Bullard's Best, Book 9
Bullard's Battle, Books 1–2
Bullard's Battle, Books 3–4
Bullard's Battle, Books 5–6
Bullard's Battle, Books 7–8

Terkel's Team
Damon's Deal, Book 1

Wade's War, Book 2
Gage's Goal, Book 3
Calum's Contact, Book 4
Rick's Road, Book 5
Scott's Summit, Book 6
Brody's Beast, Book 7
Terkel's Twist, Book 8
Terkel's Triumph, Book 9

Terk's Guardians
Radar, Book 1
Legend, Book 2
Bojan, Book 3

Kate Morgan
Simon Says… Hide, Book 1
Simon Says… Jump, Book 2
Simon Says… Ride, Book 3
Simon Says… Scream, Book 4
Simon Says… Run, Book 5
Simon Says… Walk, Book 6
Simon Says… Forgive, Book 7
Simon Says… Swim, Book 8

Hathaway House
Aaron, Book 1
Brock, Book 2
Cole, Book 3
Denton, Book 4
Elliot, Book 5
Finn, Book 6
Gregory, Book 7
Heath, Book 8

Iain, Book 9
Jaden, Book 10
Keith, Book 11
Lance, Book 12
Melissa, Book 13
Nash, Book 14
Owen, Book 15
Percy, Book 16
Quinton, Book 17
Ryatt, Book 18
Spencer, Book 19
Timothy, Book 20
Urban, Book 21
Victor, Book 22
Hathaway House, Books 1–3
Hathaway House, Books 4–6
Hathaway House, Books 7–9

The K9 Files
Ethan, Book 1
Pierce, Book 2
Zane, Book 3
Blaze, Book 4
Lucas, Book 5
Parker, Book 6
Carter, Book 7
Weston, Book 8
Greyson, Book 9
Rowan, Book 10
Caleb, Book 11
Kurt, Book 12
Tucker, Book 13

Harley, Book 14
Kyron, Book 15
Jenner, Book 16
Rhys, Book 17
Landon, Book 18
Harper, Book 19
Kascius, Book 20
Declan, Book 21
Bauer, Book 22
The K9 Files, Books 1–2
The K9 Files, Books 3–4
The K9 Files, Books 5–6
The K9 Files, Books 7–8
The K9 Files, Books 9–10
The K9 Files, Books 11–12

Lovely Lethal Gardens

Arsenic in the Azaleas, Book 1
Bones in the Begonias, Book 2
Corpse in the Carnations, Book 3
Daggers in the Dahlias, Book 4
Evidence in the Echinacea, Book 5
Footprints in the Ferns, Book 6
Gun in the Gardenias, Book 7
Handcuffs in the Heather, Book 8
Ice Pick in the Ivy, Book 9
Jewels in the Juniper, Book 10
Killer in the Kiwis, Book 11
Lifeless in the Lilies, Book 12
Murder in the Marigolds, Book 13
Nabbed in the Nasturtiums, Book 14
Offed in the Orchids, Book 15

Poison in the Pansies, Book 16
Quarry in the Quince, Book 17
Revenge in the Roses, Book 18
Silenced in the Sunflowers, Book 19
Toes up in the Tulips, Book 20
Uzi in the Urn, Book 21
Victim in the Violets, Book 22
Whispers in the Wisteria, Book 23
Lovely Lethal Gardens, Books 1–2
Lovely Lethal Gardens, Books 3–4
Lovely Lethal Gardens, Books 5–6
Lovely Lethal Gardens, Books 7–8
Lovely Lethal Gardens, Books 9–10

Psychic Visions Series
Tuesday's Child
Hide 'n Go Seek
Maddy's Floor
Garden of Sorrow
Knock Knock...
Rare Find
Eyes to the Soul
Now You See Her
Shattered
Into the Abyss
Seeds of Malice
Eye of the Falcon
Itsy-Bitsy Spider
Unmasked
Deep Beneath
From the Ashes
Stroke of Death

Ice Maiden
Snap, Crackle…
What If…
Talking Bones
String of Tears
Inked Forever
Insanity
Psychic Visions Books 1–3
Psychic Visions Books 4–6
Psychic Visions Books 7–9

By Death Series
Touched by Death
Haunted by Death
Chilled by Death
By Death Books 1–3

Broken Protocols – Romantic Comedy Series
Cat's Meow
Cat's Pajamas
Cat's Cradle
Cat's Claus
Broken Protocols 1-4

Broken and... Mending
Skin
Scars
Scales (of Justice)
Broken but… Mending 1-3

Glory
Genesis
Tori

Celeste
Glory Trilogy

Biker Blues
Morgan: Biker Blues, Volume 1
Cash: Biker Blues, Volume 2

SEALs of Honor
Mason: SEALs of Honor, Book 1
Hawk: SEALs of Honor, Book 2
Dane: SEALs of Honor, Book 3
Swede: SEALs of Honor, Book 4
Shadow: SEALs of Honor, Book 5
Cooper: SEALs of Honor, Book 6
Markus: SEALs of Honor, Book 7
Evan: SEALs of Honor, Book 8
Mason's Wish: SEALs of Honor, Book 9
Chase: SEALs of Honor, Book 10
Brett: SEALs of Honor, Book 11
Devlin: SEALs of Honor, Book 12
Easton: SEALs of Honor, Book 13
Ryder: SEALs of Honor, Book 14
Macklin: SEALs of Honor, Book 15
Corey: SEALs of Honor, Book 16
Warrick: SEALs of Honor, Book 17
Tanner: SEALs of Honor, Book 18
Jackson: SEALs of Honor, Book 19
Kanen: SEALs of Honor, Book 20
Nelson: SEALs of Honor, Book 21
Taylor: SEALs of Honor, Book 22
Colton: SEALs of Honor, Book 23
Troy: SEALs of Honor, Book 24
Axel: SEALs of Honor, Book 25

Baylor: SEALs of Honor, Book 26
Hudson: SEALs of Honor, Book 27
Lachlan: SEALs of Honor, Book 28
Paxton: SEALs of Honor, Book 29
Bronson: SEALs of Honor, Book 30
Hale: SEALs of Honor, Book 31
SEALs of Honor, Books 1–3
SEALs of Honor, Books 4–6
SEALs of Honor, Books 7–10
SEALs of Honor, Books 11–13
SEALs of Honor, Books 14–16
SEALs of Honor, Books 17–19
SEALs of Honor, Books 20–22
SEALs of Honor, Books 23–25

Heroes for Hire
Levi's Legend: Heroes for Hire, Book 1
Stone's Surrender: Heroes for Hire, Book 2
Merk's Mistake: Heroes for Hire, Book 3
Rhodes's Reward: Heroes for Hire, Book 4
Flynn's Firecracker: Heroes for Hire, Book 5
Logan's Light: Heroes for Hire, Book 6
Harrison's Heart: Heroes for Hire, Book 7
Saul's Sweetheart: Heroes for Hire, Book 8
Dakota's Delight: Heroes for Hire, Book 9
Tyson's Treasure: Heroes for Hire, Book 10
Jace's Jewel: Heroes for Hire, Book 11
Rory's Rose: Heroes for Hire, Book 12
Brandon's Bliss: Heroes for Hire, Book 13
Liam's Lily: Heroes for Hire, Book 14
North's Nikki: Heroes for Hire, Book 15
Anders's Angel: Heroes for Hire, Book 16

Reyes's Raina: Heroes for Hire, Book 17
Dezi's Diamond: Heroes for Hire, Book 18
Vince's Vixen: Heroes for Hire, Book 19
Ice's Icing: Heroes for Hire, Book 20
Johan's Joy: Heroes for Hire, Book 21
Galen's Gemma: Heroes for Hire, Book 22
Zack's Zest: Heroes for Hire, Book 23
Bonaparte's Belle: Heroes for Hire, Book 24
Noah's Nemesis: Heroes for Hire, Book 25
Tomas's Trials: Heroes for Hire, Book 26
Carson's Choice: Heroes for Hire, Book 27
Dante's Decision: Heroes for Hire, Book 28
Steven's Solace: Heroes for Hire, Book 29
Heroes for Hire, Books 1–3
Heroes for Hire, Books 4–6
Heroes for Hire, Books 7–9
Heroes for Hire, Books 10–12
Heroes for Hire, Books 13–15
Heroes for Hire, Books 16–18
Heroes for Hire, Books 19–21
Heroes for Hire, Books 22–24

SEALs of Steel

Badger: SEALs of Steel, Book 1
Erick: SEALs of Steel, Book 2
Cade: SEALs of Steel, Book 3
Talon: SEALs of Steel, Book 4
Laszlo: SEALs of Steel, Book 5
Geir: SEALs of Steel, Book 6
Jager: SEALs of Steel, Book 7
The Final Reveal: SEALs of Steel, Book 8
SEALs of Steel, Books 1–4

SEALs of Steel, Books 5–8
SEALs of Steel, Books 1–8

The Mavericks
Kerrick, Book 1
Griffin, Book 2
Jax, Book 3
Beau, Book 4
Asher, Book 5
Ryker, Book 6
Miles, Book 7
Nico, Book 8
Keane, Book 9
Lennox, Book 10
Gavin, Book 11
Shane, Book 12
Diesel, Book 13
Jerricho, Book 14
Killian, Book 15
Hatch, Book 16
Corbin, Book 17
Aiden, Book 18
The Mavericks, Books 1–2
The Mavericks, Books 3–4
The Mavericks, Books 5–6
The Mavericks, Books 7–8
The Mavericks, Books 9–10
The Mavericks, Books 11–12

Standalone Novellas
It's a Dog's Life
Riana's Revenge
Second Chances

Published Young Adult Books:

Family Blood Ties Series

Vampire in Denial

Vampire in Distress

Vampire in Design

Vampire in Deceit

Vampire in Defiance

Vampire in Conflict

Vampire in Chaos

Vampire in Crisis

Vampire in Control

Vampire in Charge

Family Blood Ties Set 1–3

Family Blood Ties Set 1–5

Family Blood Ties Set 4–6

Family Blood Ties Set 7–9

Sian's Solution, A Family Blood Ties Series Prequel
   Novelette

Design series

Dangerous Designs

Deadly Designs

Darkest Designs

Design Series Trilogy

Standalone

In Cassie's Corner

Gem Stone (a Gemma Stone Mystery)

Time Thieves

Published Non-Fiction Books:

Career Essentials
Career Essentials: The Résumé
Career Essentials: The Cover Letter
Career Essentials: The Interview
Career Essentials: 3 in 1

9 781773 367835